"What in hell are you doing wandering around out here?" Forest asked, his face a tight mask of anger.

"I...I heard something," Julie said. As his gaze traveled the length of her, she was all too conscious of the shortness of her T-shirt, the way the thin material stretched taut across her breasts.

He grabbed hold of her arm, his grip hot, almost fevered, his eyes emanating a near-madness that frightened her. "And what did you hear?"

"I heard someone crying...a little boy." A chill shivered up her back, and she twisted out of his grip and stepped away from him. "You heard it, too, didn't you? Who is it, Forest? Who did I hear?" she asked softly.

"You just got your first introduction to the ghost of Kingsdon Hill." A smile twisted his lips, a bloodless smile that caused her to take another step backward. "Welcome to hell, Julie."

Dear Reader,

Wow! You're really going to love our offering this month, and who can blame you? We've got a terrific book waiting for you, so let me start right off by telling you about it.

Carla Cassidy is back. This favorite author checks in with *Mystery Child,* a haunting tale of the persistence—and unreliability—of memory. But finding out the truth becomes imperative for heroine Julie Kingsdon. She needs to know whether her brother-in-law, Forest Kingsdon, is a threat to her son and her sanity—or their savior.

It's a very spooky, special book, taking a look at the dark side of love. And you can only find it here, in our Shadows.

Enjoy!

Leslie Wainger
Senior Editor and Editorial Coordinator

Please address questions and book requests to:
Silhouette Reader Service
U.S.: 3010 Walden Ave., P.O. Box 1325, Buffalo, NY 14269
Canadian: P.O. Box 609, Fort Erie, Ont. L2A 5X3

CARLA CASSIDY

Mystery
Child

Published by Silhouette Books
America's Publisher of Contemporary Romance

SILHOUETTE BOOKS

ISBN 0-373-27061-5

MYSTERY CHILD

Printed in U.S.A.

Books by Carla Cassidy

Silhouette Shadows

Swamp Secrets #4
Heart of the Beast #11
Silent Screams #25
Mystery Child #61

Silhouette Romance

Patchwork Family #818
Whatever Alex Wants... #856
Fire and Spice #884
Homespun Hearts #905
Golden Girl #924
Something New #942
Pixie Dust #958
The Littlest Matchmaker #978
The Marriage Scheme #996
Anything for Danny #1048

Silhouette Desire

A Fleeting Moment #784
Under the Boardwalk #882

Silhouette Intimate Moments

One of the Good Guys #531
Try to Remember #560
Fugitive Father #604

Silhouette Books

Silhouette Shadows Short Stories 1993
"Devil and the Deep Blue Sea"

The Loop
Getting it Right: Jessica

CARLA CASSIDY

is the author of ten young-adult novels, as well as many contemporary romances. She has been a cheerleader for the Kansas City Chiefs football team and has traveled the East Coast as a singer and dancer in a band, but the greatest pleasure she's had is in creating romance and happiness for readers.

CHAPTER ONE

No lights of welcome lit the long, narrow road that led to the house on the hill. Fog blanketed the valley below; gray, dense clouds completely covered the small town of Kingsdon, Missouri.

Julie Kingsdon edged her car to the shoulder of the narrow road and shut off the engine. Checking to make certain Bobby was still sleeping soundly in the back seat, she got out of the car. Stretching, she tried to unkink the muscles that had tensed up during the last two days of driving.

She took a deep breath and released it slowly, then leaned against the front bumper of the car. She needed to collect her thoughts before advancing the rest of the way up the hill to the house that belonged to her dead husband's brother.

She pulled her sweater more tightly around her, unsure if the chill that danced up her spine was a result of the cool, autumn-evening air or the reality of facing the unknown.

The unknown. Her gaze once again went to Kingsdon Manor. It was an architectural anachronism. Its gray stones and turret rooms belonged to another place, another time, certainly not on a hilltop in southern Missouri.

A rooster weather vane, incongruent with the design of the house, clung to one of the roof steeples, spinning chaotically in the late-evening breeze. The windows yawned darkly, as if ready to swallow anyone who ventured near. Even the golden hues of twilight couldn't chase away the forbidding shadows that surrounded the house.

Julie had driven halfway across the country to get here and had no idea what she would find. The only thing she knew for certain was that she needed to be here. She and her son had nowhere else to go.

With another shiver, she got back into the car, wondering if coming had been a mistake. Perhaps she should have just stayed in New York City, continued the daily struggle to survive.

She gripped the steering wheel in grim determination. No, she'd had to come here. She needed to meet her late husband's brother. It was important that Bobby meet the only relative he had besides her. And in any case, this was Bobby's heritage. She had every right to claim it for him.

She looked over her shoulder, to where her son slept, his arms wrapped tightly around the scraggly stuffed dog that he'd slept with every night for the past seven years. Sweet Bobby. Her heart softened as she gazed at his mahogany hair tousled into disarray, his cheeks ruddy with color. The last year had been so difficult for him, for them both.

Now it was time to go. She started the engine. As she drove up the lane, her heart thudded in frenzied anticipation. What sort of welcome could they expect? She had written several letters to Forest Kingsdon, detailing her desire to come and introduce Bobby to him, but she'd received no reply. Not that she'd really expected any. Forest hadn't come to Jeffrey's funeral, nor had he sent any note of sympathy. Julie didn't know what had caused the rift years ago between Jeffrey and his younger brother, but whatever it was, even death hadn't breached it.

She shoved the memory of her husband out of her mind, thoughts of him spearing through her with a myriad of raw emotions—pain, loss and always the sharp stab of guilt.

Pulling the car up in front of the house, she shut off the engine and stared out the window. It was even more forbidding up close. The fog had made its way up the hill, consuming the first level of the house in ghostly breath. The pale glow from interior lights changed the fog to an eerie yellowish green.

Jeffrey hadn't prepared her for the decayed grandeur of his ancestral home. Nor had he mentioned the utter isolation. Julie opened her door, the misty night air embracing her once again as she slid out of the car. The house sat by itself, surrounded by thick woods. She stood for a moment, listening to the cacophony of insect songs. It was pleasant, almost lulling, and she felt a burst of optimism. Everything was going to be okay, she told herself firmly. It was right that she had come.

Opening the back door, she lifted Bobby in her arms, not surprised when he didn't waken. Instead he curled his little body into the contours of hers and wrapped his legs around her waist. His breathing remained deep, regular in the rhythm of slumber. The child could sleep through an atomic war, she thought with a smile. It wouldn't be long before he'd be too big for her to carry. She breathed in his little-boy scent, her heart once again expanding with love.

She was worried about her son, who'd had difficulty adjusting to life without his father. In the last couple of months he'd been too somber, too quiet, and he'd regressed, relinquishing his seven-year-old independence for the clinging stage he'd gone through when he was younger. The psychologist had suggested that what the boy needed was a sense of connection to something or someone other than Julie. She hoped this visit to Kingsdon Manor would fill the void left by Jeffrey's absence. She wished she had family of her own that could rally around, but there was nobody. Jeffrey and Bobby had been her family, and now Jeffrey was gone.

She walked up the steps onto the large front porch, the weathered wood creaking ominously beneath her weight. She didn't see a doorbell and so knocked on the massive door, the sound echoing in the stillness of the night. She shifted Bobby from one hip to the other, her nerves suddenly raw as she waited for the door to be answered. The optimism that had filled her only moments before seeped away, like helium from a pin-pricked balloon.

Maybe this was all a big mistake, Julie thought. Maybe Jeffrey had shut his brother out of his life for a very good reason. Part of her had a sudden urge to turn and run. But she fought the impulse and knocked again on the door, this time more forcefully. She hadn't driven halfway across the United States to turn coward at the last minute. She couldn't have closure, couldn't move forward with her life until she resolved some of the issues Jeffrey's death had left behind. She hadn't realized how little she actually knew about Jeffrey until she'd had to go through his paperwork after his death. And they'd been married for a little over eight years. Despite everything, half of this house belonged to her, as Jeffrey's widow, and Bobby.

As the front door creaked open, she straightened her shoulders with determination. "What do you want?" A churlish masculine voice issued forth from the tall, dark form in the shadowed doorway.

"I'm—I'm here to see Forest Kingsdon." Julie took a step forward, trying not to be intimidated by the broad shoulders, the daunting height, the shrouded features of the man before her.

"What for?" There was no attempt at civility in his brusque voice, and yet there was an odd familiarity in the tone. He flipped on a dim porch light, and as the thin glow fell on his features, she knew she was face-to-face with her husband's brother.

For a brief moment a flash of pain exploded in her as she gazed at him. He looked so like Jeffrey had when she had first met him nine years ago. At that time she'd been full of eagerness, anxious for the intimacy of marriage to chase away her loneliness.

"What do you want?" he repeated, a tinge of impatience in his deep voice.

"I'm Julie, Jeffrey's wife. I wrote to you several times." She hesitated a moment, then continued, "You never answered my letters."

"No, I didn't." No apology. No regret colored his succinct words.

Julie shifted Bobby's weight, and she saw Forest's eyes narrow, as if he was noticing the boy for the first time. He released a weighty sigh and opened the door. "Come in," he said, his voice weary with resignation.

She followed him through a large hallway and into a room where a fire snapped and crackled, producing an inviting barrier against the chill of the night. "You can put him down there," he said, gesturing toward a richly colored brocade sofa.

Julie relinquished the sleeping child to the comfort of the couch, relieved to rest her tired arms. She stood uncertainly, watching as Forest settled into a chair near the fireplace, his gaze absorbed by the flames dancing on the grate.

With the light of the fire shining on his face, she saw that his initial resemblance to Jeffrey had been merely an illusion. There was a certain likeness, but she remembered Jeffrey's face as being softer, as if a sculptor had practiced on him before perfecting the harsh beauty of the man before her.

Forest Kingsdon's hair was a dark shock hanging well over the collar of his denim shirt. The lower portion of his face was darkly shadowed with a growth of whiskers. Jeffrey had been attractive in a refined, dignified sort of way. But this man was devastating in an uncivilized, primitive fashion. There was a whisper of cruelty in his harsh features, and Julie found herself both repelled by and oddly drawn to him.

"Why are you here? Why have you come?" He didn't look at her, but continued staring at the fire.

She moved over to the wing chair opposite him and sat down. "There are several reasons why I've come," she finally hedged.

He turned and looked at her, his dark eyes reflecting the fire's blaze. There was no softness in his expression, no hint of welcome or acceptance. "Give me one good one."

Julie stiffened at the command in his tone. "As Jeffrey's widow, I inherited half of this house."

He nodded, his lips twisting into a bitter parody of a smile. "Ah, yes. Congratulations." The smile immediately dissipated. He stood up abruptly. "You've had a long journey. I'll take you to the rooms you and the boy can use for the night."

"His name is Bobby," she said pointedly as she stood up. She wasn't sure what she'd expected from Jeffrey's brother, but it certainly wasn't this cold bitterness. She'd hoped to find a home here for themselves. She'd hoped that Forest Kingsdon would be a loving uncle to Bobby and a friend to her.

Tears burned in her eyes and made her realize the extent of her exhaustion. She'd just driven twelve hours, after a restless night in a cheap motel. Surely things would look brighter in the morning after a good night's sleep.

She leaned down and picked up the sleeping child, comforted by his sweet warmth. She and Bobby would be fine...with or without Forest Kingsdon. At least for the time being they had a roof over their heads and half equity in this mausoleum. It wasn't much, but it was a beginning.

She followed Forest up a wide staircase to the second floor. He lead her silently, as if he didn't much care whether she followed him or not. The hallway upstairs was dark, but he moved with the assurance of a cat whose vision grew sharper in the darkness.

He opened a door on his right and flipped on a light switch, illuminating a large bedroom with a canopy bed. "There's a smaller room there where the boy can sleep." He pointed to an adjoining doorway. "And the bathroom is down the hallway on your left." He turned to leave.

"Forest?" His name felt odd coming from her lips. Everything about the scene was odd, like a picture slightly out of focus. He pivoted to face her, his eyes dark and enigmatic. "I hope we get an opportunity to talk...about Jeffrey. There are some things I'd like to know, need to know."

He stared at her for a long moment, then his gaze moved from her to the child sleeping in her arms. His features grew taut and his eyes narrowed once again. Julie felt a shiver of apprehension dance up her spine, and she tightened her grip on Bobby.

"You have a legal right to be here, but I'll be quite honest. I don't want you here, and as far as I'm concerned, the subject of my brother is off-limits. Let the dead rest in peace." He whirled around and disappeared into the darkness of the hallway.

Julie stared after him for a long moment, then shut the door of the bedroom, relieved to find that it locked. She gently placed Bobby on the canopied bed, then stood back and breathed deeply, fighting against the anger that swirled inside her.

Damn him, his behavior was beyond rude! Even though he obviously hadn't been expecting her, that wasn't an excuse for his discourteous conduct. He didn't want her here. He probably expected them to move on in the morning. Well, he'd be disappointed. Julie was here and she wasn't going anywhere, at least not before she got her life back together.

Perhaps he was displeased that she had come to claim her inheritance as Jeffrey's widow. After all, he'd lived here for the past nine years without interference from Jeffrey. Surely he would be more accommodating when he realized Julie wanted nothing from him except some time to stay here and heal, both emotionally and financially.

She let go of the anger and instead focused on her surroundings. It was a pleasant room, with plush navy carpeting and navy-and-cream wallpaper. The dark, wooden furniture was ornate and obviously antique. There was a masculine feel to it, and she wondered whose room it had been when Jeffrey lived here and his parents were alive.

She moved across the floor to the doorway that led to the smaller room. Turning on the light, she gasped with surprise and delight. It was as if the room had been decorated specifically with Bobby in mind. A brown corduroy bedspread covered the single bed and the sports-motif wallpaper proclaimed it distinctly boy territory.

Julie sank down on the edge of the small bed and rubbed the center of her forehead, where a headache had blossomed with potent intensity. Nothing was as she'd expected, not this house nor her brother-in-law.

Who had slept in this little boy's room? The wallpaper and furnishings, although not new, didn't look old enough to have been either Jeffrey's or Forest's.

What had happened that had torn the brothers apart to such an extent that Forest had no desire to befriend her or Jeffrey's son? Julie wondered. And what caused the haunted, tormented look in Forest's eyes? For a moment, as he'd stared at Bobby, he'd looked just like Jeffrey had when one of his black moods had descended.

She shivered and went back into the large bedroom, where Bobby remained sleeping peacefully on the bed. She would let him stay here with her for the night. He might be frightened if he awakened in the unfamiliar room next-door.

It was then she realized she'd left their suitcases in the car. Oh well, they could make do for tonight, and she would get their things in the morning.

She pulled off Bobby's shoes and socks, then tucked him beneath the blankets of the bed, grateful that he wore comfortable jogging pants instead of jeans.

She kicked off her own jeans, then pulled off her sweater. The T-shirt beneath would make an adequate, though short nightgown. She reached beneath the shirt and unsnapped her bra, then maneuvered the straps down and pulled it through an armhole. She smiled, remembering how astonished Jeffrey had been the first time she'd removed her bra in this unconventional way. That had been early in their marriage, when she'd still believed he could fill all the dark corners of her heart. She hadn't yet known that he was incapable of the kind of emotional closeness, the intimacy she so desired. It had taken her years of marriage to realize he would never be able to give her what she wanted. There was a part of himself he always kept separate from her, a shield that guarded him and didn't allow her inside.

Shoving these painful thoughts aside, she turned out the light, then made her way to the bed. Sliding beneath the covers, she released a deep sigh, her mind filling with visions of Forest Kingsdon. She knew he was thirty-eight years old... six years younger than Jeffrey. She knew his birthday was October 20. She'd gleaned odd little details about him from Jeffrey over their years of marriage, but nothing substantial, nothing to tell her what kind of man he was in his heart.

What she hadn't expected was his overt masculinity, the dark attractiveness that had instantly caused heat to unfurl in her stomach.

She shivered as she remembered that momentary darkness in his eyes as he'd stared at Bobby. She had a sudden feeling that coming here had been a horrible mistake, but there was nothing she could do about it now. She and Bobby were here, and for at least a while, they would just have to make the best of things.

Forest Kingsdon gasped convulsively and swallowed back the yell that clogged his throat. He sat up, his body drenched in sweat. Oh, God. He'd had the nightmare... again. He ran his hands across his face, his heart filled with a bleak horror. He hadn't had one in months, had thought he'd finally left them behind. But this one had been just like all the others, tormenting him, tearing him apart.

Drawing in a deep breath, he threw the blankets aside and got out of bed. Padding to the window, he stared out at the thick woods, his heartbeat slowing to a more natural rhythm.

It was just after midnight, and the fog had thickened, like witches' soup poured over the landscape. He shivered, wishing—demanding—the last remnants of the dream to leave him, but they clung as tenaciously as did the fog to the base of the trees.

He knew why the dream had returned. The presence of Jeffrey's widow and child had stirred the remains of the past, allowed it to rise like death's breath from an open grave. And the past frightened Forest. It frightened him as nothing else could.

They should never have come here.

He leaned his head against the cool panes of the window. He knew from experience that sleep would remain distant for some time.

Julie Kingsdon . . . Jeffrey's wife. Jeffrey's widow, he reminded himself, pain spearing through him at the thought of his older brother. When he'd first received letters from Julie, telling him of her wish to come here, he'd thought he would discourage her through silence. He'd figured that if he didn't answer her letters, she wouldn't come.

She'd surprised him, first by coming, then by her physical appearance. Forest had expected somebody older, more sophisticated. With her cloud of long brown hair and the sprinkling of freckles on the bridge of her nose, Julie Kingsdon looked little more than a teenager.

And yet he'd sensed a streak of strength in her, a backbone of fortitude that would make forcing her to leave difficult. But he had to make her go. She *had* to take her son and leave, run from here as fast as she could. His dream had been an omen...a forecast of danger. They weren't safe here.

"Daddy. Daddy!"

The little boy's voice was filled with pain. It cut through Julie's sleep, pulled her from her dreams. She awakened and immediately turned toward Bobby. She swallowed her words of comfort as she saw him sleeping soundly.

She frowned and sat up, bewildered for a moment. Had the voice been part of her dream? It had sounded so real, seemed so vivid. She swung her legs over the side of the bed and stood up. She walked to the window, where the moonlight shimmered in, painting the room in streaks of pale illumination.

The childish voice had been filled with fear, the cry that of a terrified little boy. If it was a dream, what on earth had made her conjure up such a thing? She looked at Bobby once again, wondering if her worry over her son had somehow manifested itself in her dream world. It probably had.

She turned away from the window, knowing she should go back to bed, but she felt too wired for sleep. Her mouth was cotton dry. She needed a glass of water; however, she didn't like the thought of wandering around the strange house in the middle of the night

looking for the kitchen. Forest had said the bathroom was just down the hallway to the left.

Cautiously, she unlocked the bedroom door and
eased it open. The hallway was pitch-black. The house
was profoundly silent. She ran her hand along the wall
to guide herself. She walked a short distance and her
fingers encountered a doorframe, then the cool brass
of a knob. She opened the door and took a single step
inside.

She stopped, her breath immediately caught in her
chest as she saw Forest standing in the moonlight at
the window. He was naked, and there was a primitive, stark beauty in the masculine lines of his back,
the muscled strength of his legs. For a moment she was
frozen by the sight. He didn't seem to feel her presence, for he stood still.

Although his back was in shadow, there was enough
light in the room for her to see the perfect symmetry
of his physique. The broad expanse of his shoulders
was emphasized by the leanness of his waist and hips.
His buttocks were taut and his legs were long and
muscular.

Her breath pressed tightly against her rib cage as she
stared at his magnificent nakedness. She backed out
of the room and silently closed the door, then leaned
against the wall and willed her breathing to come naturally.

She closed her eyes, trying to shut away the vision
of his masculine beauty, but it seemed burned into her
brain cells. His back had been firmly muscled, a dark
expanse of flesh that had looked both warm and inviting. She swallowed hard, her mouth achingly dry.

Her blood felt thick, hot as it flowed through her veins, and she knew that, as crazy as it was, the sight of Forest had reawakened heated thoughts and hormones long dormant.

She shook her head in an attempt to dispel the mental image. She opened her eyes and scoffed inwardly. She was acting like a sexually deprived woman. She started to move down the hallway, but froze as she heard the distinct sound of a child sobbing. It was louder now, echoing in the darkness of the hallway—a pitiful sound that mournfully wrapped itself around her heart.

She stifled a scream as Forest's door flew open and he collided with her. He expelled a curse, steadying her with his hands. To her relief, he'd thrown on a pair of jeans, covering the nakedness that had so disturbed her moments before. However, she was all too aware of his chest, broad and naked save for the curling dark hair that matted the center, then trailed downward in a narrow path that disappeared into the low waist of his jeans.

He released her shoulders and reached back to flip on the bedroom light. "What in the hell are you doing out here wandering around?" he asked, his face a tight mask of anger.

"I...I heard something," she said. As his gaze traveled the length of her, she was embarrassingly conscious of the shortness of her T-shirt, the way the thin material stretched taut across her breasts. She folded her arms protectively.

"And what did you hear?" he asked, his eyes dark and enigmatic as they focused once again on her face.

"I heard someone crying...a little boy." She flushed, realizing how ridiculous it sounded.

His eyes flared in something like surprise and he grabbed hold of her arm, his grip hot, feeling almost fevered. "What exactly did you hear?"

He stood too close to her, his body radiating heat, his eyes emanating a near madness that frightened her. "I—I heard a boy crying for his daddy. It woke me up."

"Perhaps it was a dream." He spoke the words flatly, as if he didn't really expect her to believe them.

"That's what I thought at first, but I heard it again...just a minute ago. A little boy sobbing." A chill shivered up her back, and she twisted out of his grip and stepped away from him. "You heard it, too. Didn't you?" She stared at him. "Is that what brought you out of your room?"

He hesitated, then nodded. "I thought it might be your boy. I thought perhaps he'd woken up and was wandering around the house in the dark, afraid."

She shook her head. "Bobby is sound asleep." She licked her lips nervously, wishing he would step back from her. His nearness was disturbing. "Who is it? Do you have a child?"

A wave of bitterness suffused his face, and his eyes, haunted with shadows, grew darker. "No. There's no child here except your son."

"Then whom did I hear?" she asked softly.

A smile twisted his lips, a horrible, bloodless smile that caused Julie to take another step backward. "You just got your introduction to the ghost of Kingsdon Hill. Welcome to hell."

CHAPTER TWO

"Mom?" One of Julie's eyelids was pulled open by a little finger. "Are you awake? Mom?" She groaned, still unaccustomed to this method of greeting a new day. "Mom, is this Uncle Forest's house?"

Bobby's question drove the last of her sleep away as she remembered the strange events of the night before. She sat up and shoved her hair out of her eyes, smiling at the little boy sprawled on his stomach next to her.

"Good morning, champ," she said, reaching out to smooth a lock of his dark hair away from his forehead. "Yes, this is your uncle Forest's house. You were sound asleep when we arrived last night."

Julie looked around, surprised to see their suitcases lined up just inside the door. She frowned. How had they gotten there? It was obvious Forest had retrieved them from the car, but when had he put them in here?

"Bobby, your bedroom is through that doorway." Julie pointed to the smaller, connecting room. "Why don't you take your suitcase and unpack your things?"

"Okay." He bounded from the bed with the enthusiastic energy of a seven-year-old. It was an encouraging change from his recent listlessness. He grabbed his suitcase and lugged it across the floor and into the next bedroom. Julie smiled when she heard his exclamation of delight as he entered the little room. It sounded good. He'd been too sober, too quiet since Jeffrey's accident and death.

She flopped back on the bed, her mind whirling with the events of the night before. After making his startling announcement about the ghost of Kingsdon Hill, Forest had turned and gone back into his room, leaving her stunned and frightened in the dark hallway.

With the light of morning streaming through the windows, chasing away the lingering shadows of night, his words about a ghost seemed ridiculous. More than likely what she had heard was Bobby. It wouldn't be the first time the little boy had moaned or cried out in his sleep.

She stretched, feeling surprisingly rested despite the interruption of her sleep in the middle of the night. She was suddenly anxious to get up and explore the house—acquaint herself with the place that had been Jeffrey's home.

It was nearly an hour later when she and Bobby made their way down the wide staircase, both showered and hungry. They followed the scent of fresh-brewed coffee and fried bacon through the living room and into a large kitchen, where a slender old woman stood at the stove with her back to them.

"Good morning," Julie said.

The woman whirled around, her wrinkled face wreathed in a huge smile. "Ah, there you are! Forest told me we had guests." She moved closer to Bobby and bent down, her smile warm and welcoming. "My, you're the spitting image of your father."

"You knew my daddy?" Bobby asked in surprise.

"Indeed I did. I'm Lottie Currothers, and I raised your father from the time he was a baby, spanked his butt more times than I care to admit."

Bobby smiled shyly, and Julie realized that perhaps this woman held the answers to the thousands of questions that plagued her.

"Here, sit down." She gestured to a round oak table where two place settings awaited them. "If you're anything like your father was, you'll eat at least a dozen of my hotcakes." She placed a plate of golden pancakes on the table, then looked at them both expectantly. "Eat," she commanded.

Julie helped Bobby fill his plate and pour syrup, watching as the old woman busied herself at the stove. "You've been here a long time, Mrs. Currothers?" she asked.

"Please, call me Lottie. Everyone does." She poured Julie a cup of coffee, then joined them at the table. "I lived here for thirty years...until Jeffrey left. In the last ten years I've come in and done the cooking and a little housework, although Forest is pretty self-reliant."

"I'm sure he is," Julie replied dryly, thinking of Jeffrey's brother. "Where is Forest this morning?"

"He's a very early riser. He already had his breakfast and left for his morning walk." Lottie turned her attention to Bobby, who was in the process of polishing off his pancakes. "That's what I like to see, a boy with a healthy appetite."

"These pancakes are good," Bobby said, a glob of syrup dripping from his chin. Julie used her napkin to wipe it off, smiling when he squirmed away from her and resumed eating.

"If you like those, wait until you get a taste of my homemade cinnamon rolls. They were always your daddy's favorite," Lottie said.

"Then they'll be my favorite, too!" Bobby proclaimed. For a moment his bottom lip quivered ominously, and Julie feared tears for the loss of his father would follow. However, he looked at Lottie, drew in a deep breath and smiled bravely at his mother, then focused his attention back on the last of his pancakes.

Julie realized the questions she wanted to ask the older woman about Jeffrey would have to be posed later, at a time when Bobby wasn't present. His grief over his father's tragic death was still too raw, too painful.

"I didn't get to see much last night when we arrived, but from what I did see, this is a marvelous house," Julie said to Lottie.

The old woman's brown eyes sparkled and she nodded, a soft smile easing the deep wrinkles on her face. "Ah, yes, it's a wonderful house. It was built almost a hundred years ago by Gabriel Kingsdon." She looked at Bobby and her smile deepened. "That would have been your great-grandfather. They say he was a brilliant, ambitious man. He came here and built this house. He opened a sawmill down in the valley. The town of Kingsdon grew up around the mill."

"Wow," Bobby said, obviously impressed that there was a town named after not only his great-grandfather, but himself as well. Julie knew at that moment that this trip had been worthwhile. Bobby needed to know his roots, and she had none of her own to offer him. "Can we go see the sawmill, Mom?" he asked, showing the boyish eagerness that had been sadly lacking in recent months.

"I don't know, honey. We'll see."

"Next week there's the fall festival, a big celebration down at the mill. You'll want to go to that. Everyone attends," Lottie said. Again her gaze fell on Bobby. "There's all kinds of races and contests for kids, and enough food to feed the people in four counties."

"Ah, Mom, we've got to go to that," Bobby exclaimed.

"We'll see, Bobby," Julie said again absently. "Whatever made Jeffrey leave all this behind and move to New York City?" she asked.

The friendly sparkle in Lottie's eyes was immediately doused. "I wouldn't know nothing about that," she said stiffly as she turned back to the stove.

A ripple of unease crawled up Julie's spine.

"Mom?" Bobby looked at her uncertainly, as if he sensed her disquiet.

She patted his arm and smiled reassuringly. "When did you say this festival was?"

"Next Saturday." Lottie turned back around and smiled, although her face had a remoteness that hadn't been there moments ago. "It's a whole day of fun for young and old alike."

"We gotta go, Mom."

"Go where?" Forest Kingsdon appeared in the doorway.

Both Julie and Bobby jumped at the unexpected sound of the deep voice. "Land's sakes," Lottie exclaimed with a hand over her heart. "I ought to box your ears, sneaking up on us like that." She began clearing the dishes from the table. Julie rose automatically to help. "Just sit yourself back down," Lottie protested firmly. "I reckon if I can cook it, I can clean it up." Julie hesitated with her plate in her hand, then finally sat again.

Forest walked across the kitchen, filling the room with his sheer masculinity. He was dressed in a pair of worn jeans and a red flannel shirt that emphasized the width of his shoulders. In the bright sunshine that filled the kitchen, Julie wondered how she'd thought for a single moment that he looked anything like Jeffrey. Forest was bigger, more vital, more primal than Jeffrey had ever been.

Forest poured himself a cup of coffee, then leaned against the cabinet, a smile curling one corner of his mouth. "Lottie is quite territorial about her kitchen," he observed.

Julie said nothing, thinking that the old woman had probably learned about being territorial from him. He'd certainly been unfriendly last night about sharing his domain. For an instant her mind filled with a vision of him standing naked before his bedroom window. Heat swept into her cheeks and she cleared her throat self-consciously. "Lottie was just telling us some of the history of the house," she said. "From what I saw last night, it's quite a beautiful place."

"Are you my uncle?" Bobby asked, apparently unable to contain his curiosity as he stared up at the tall man.

"I suppose I am." He sipped his coffee. His gaze landed on Bobby, then immediately moved back to Julie. "You're welcome to explore the house. However, I'd prefer that you stay away from the basement. That's my workroom, and it wouldn't be safe for the boy."

"His name is Bobby," Julie returned tightly.

He drained his coffee and handed the cup to Lottie. "I've got to get to the mill." He strode out of the kitchen.

Julie immediately jumped up. "You stay here and finish your milk," she said to Bobby. Then she followed Forest, catching up with him as he reached the wide staircase. "Forest?"

He turned and stared at her. He'd thought she'd looked young the night before, but this morning in the full sunshine he noted the lines that radiated out from the corners of her eyes, lines that proclaimed her to be older...and a woman who smiled often. However, she wasn't smiling now. Her lips were compressed in a tight line and her brown eyes sparked with yellow flecks of angry fire.

"You asked me last night to give you one good reason why I'd come here. That boy in there is my good reason." Her words were clipped, filled with suppressed emotion and an unconcealed dislike. "Nine months ago he lost his father in a tragic car accident.

He's frightened and lonely, and right now he needs more than I can give him. I don't know what happened years ago between you and Jeffrey, but that doesn't matter. I don't want your money. I'm not here to interfere in your life. We just need some time, and Bobby needs a connection to his father's brother. He desperately needs you.''

Each one of her words bit into him like the ferocious teeth of a vicious dog, reminding him of another time, another boy...a boy whose cries now tormented his dreams, twisted his soul, haunted this house. Forest knew Julie was attempting to appeal to his heart. What she didn't know was that he had no heart. Inside his chest was a ball of bitterness that ate at him day and night, and a misery of guilt that weighed him down like a mountain.

He looked down at her, reluctantly admiring the steely strength in her eyes, the determination that stiffened her shoulders. ''I'm sorry. I have nothing to give to him.'' Without waiting for her to speak again, he turned and went upstairs.

Minutes later he left the house, walking out into the cool morning air and heading for the path that led through the woods, eventually winding its way to the back entrance of the sawmill.

As he walked along the dirt trail, the sky disappeared behind huge tree limbs and leafy canopies. A chill permeated him, the natural crispness of the forest in autumn, the unnatural cold that had been with him for ten long years. He could have driven his car to the mill, but walking through the woods was his penance, a self-imposed punishment for past transgressions.

Had he been a stronger man, he would have taken his own life long ago, ended the nightmares, the inner turmoil that afflicted him. However, part of him would not allow such an escape. Death would be too easy, would be far too good for him.

As always when he reached a certain fallen tree, he paused and allowed his mind to skip back to a distant time. He sat down on the thick trunk and covered his face with his hands.

The woods suddenly came alive with the sounds of boyish laughter, childish mirth that momentarily filled Forest's soul. "Come find me! I'm hiding!" The child's voice expanded in his head, followed by giggles that drew an answering smile to his lips. He allowed the auditory memory to play through him, like a healing balm on deep wounds.

A bird overhead crowed raucously and the memory faded, leaving him empty, bereft. He groaned and tore his hands from his face, looking around wildly, as if he could make the memory become reality by sheer willpower alone. But of course, he couldn't.

"Come on, Mom," Bobby clambered up the narrow stairs that led to the third floor of the old house.

"Bobby, wait up, I don't think we should—"

"Aw, Mom, you heard Uncle Forest. He said we could explore." Bobby paused and turned to look at her impatiently. "He said we shouldn't go down to his workroom, but he didn't say nothing about upstairs."

"Anything." Julie automatically corrected her son, who sighed in exasperation.

"Whatever," he answered. He danced from one foot to the other, waiting for her to catch up with him.

They had been exploring the house most of the day. After Forest had left for the mill, Julie had silently seethed a good part of the morning. Lottie's sudden unfriendliness when she'd asked about Jeffrey and Forest's coldness had left her confused and upset.

She and Bobby had finished their unpacking, then had begun the adventure of investigating the nooks and crannies of the house. It had taken them the entire morning just to explore the first floor, which included the large living room, the kitchen, a library, a formal dining room and a small office. They'd eaten lunch, then moved to the second floor, where they'd discovered six bedrooms and three baths. It was nearing suppertime now, and Bobby was determined that they finish their exploration of the third floor before it was time to eat. Julie was pleased by his curiosity, the enthusiasm he seemed to draw from merely being in these surroundings.

"Wow, look at all of this stuff," Bobby exclaimed when he opened the door at the top of the stairs and walked into a large room. Shrouded furniture, antique trunks, unmarked boxes—remnants of lifetimes were contained here. Julie batted at a cobweb as she followed her son, who blazed a trail through the room, stopping here and there to exclaim over a particular item.

She climbed over a stack of boxes and found Bobby staring at his reflection in an antique mirror, the glass distorted and warped. "See how funny I look?" he said with a giggle, pointing to the squat, fat image before him. His giggles increased when she stood next to him.

A moment later he was off again, exploring further. His footsteps stirred the fine layer of dust and sent it floating in the air.

"Come on, Bobby," Julie said, stifling a cough. "It's too dusty up here." She walked back toward the doorway.

"Mom, come and look at this."

"Bobby, I don't think we should be up here," she said. There was something sad about this room of boxes and castoffs. She wondered if any of Jeffrey's things were here. When he had left this house, had the items he'd left behind been boxed up and relegated to dust and cobwebs? A chill suddenly touched her as she realized the attic held a definite unnatural iciness. "Come on, Bobby."

"Mom, please! Just come and look at this. You gotta see it!" There was awe in Bobby's voice, and with a sigh, Julie wove her way to where he stood. Before him was a rocking horse. Not an ordinary rocking horse. This one was quite large, and obviously hand carved. It was breathtaking. A wild stallion with flaring nostrils and powerful haunches, it looked as if it might snort and bolt across the room at any moment.

"Oh, it's beautiful," Julie breathed softly. She ran her hand lightly across the flowing wooden mane, her fingers disturbing the sheen of dust.

"Who do you think it belongs to?" Bobby asked.

"I don't know. Perhaps it was your uncle's, or your father's." It was impossible to tell the age of the piece. It might have been a hundred years old, or it could have been carved more recently. The dust that coated it was the only visible sign of age.

"You think Uncle Forest would let me use it?" Bobby asked.

"You're too old for rocking horses," Julie said, guiding him away from the horse and back toward the stairs.

"Not that one. Did you see how big it was?"

"Ah, there you are." Lottie greeted them as they descended the staircase. "I thought you might like to know supper will be ready in about fifteen minutes."

"Oh, thank you, Lottie. We'll wash up and be right down." Julie hesitated, noticing the necklace around the older woman's neck. "What a beautiful piece of jewelry," she said as she stepped forward to get a closer look.

"I've had it for years and years," Lottie said, holding out the filigreed-gold heart. "It used to have a heart-shaped ruby hanging from the bottom, but it fell off somewhere years ago. I never found it."

"That's a shame, but it's still a beautiful necklace." Julie touched Bobby's shoulder. "Come on, sport. Let's go wash the dust off before we go downstairs to eat."

"You might use the bathroom at the far end of the hall on the right. Forest came in just a few minutes ago and he always heads right to the shower," Lottie said.

Julie thanked her for the warning and then led Bobby down the hallway. Thank goodness Lottie had told her Forest was home. All she needed was to walk in on the man while he was in the shower. One unexpected encounter with his naked body had been quite enough.

Minutes later, they went down to the kitchen, where Lottie was busy setting platters of hot food on the table. "Sit down, sit down," she instructed them. "Forest should be here in just a minute."

"Hmm, everything looks wonderful," Julie said, sliding into the chair the housekeeper indicated.

"Old Mr. Kingsdon used to say that in another life I must have been head cook for the gods," Lottie replied proudly.

"You mean Forest and Jeffrey's father?" Julie asked.

Lottie nodded. "Richard Kingsdon." Her eyes dimmed with sadness. "He died too young."

"Who?" Forest stepped into the kitchen, his body almost vibrating with tension as he looked first at Lottie, then at Julie.

"Your daddy," Lottie replied, and Forest visibly relaxed.

"How did he die?" Julie asked.

"There was an accident at the mill." Forest walked over to the table and held out a book to Julie. "I found this at the mill today and thought the boy might like to look through it. It's the history of the town of Kingsdon and the family."

"Thank you," Julie said, surprised and touched at the gesture. Perhaps there was some hope here after all, she thought. As Forest took the seat next to her, she was vividly aware of his scent, the fresh smell of the timberland mingling with the clean odor of minty soap.

For the next few minutes they filled their plates and ate in silence. Bobby's wide-eyed gaze went from his food to his uncle, and Julie knew her son was intimidated by Forest's forbidding ambience. Julie could relate to his feelings. In truth, she was rather intimidated by the tall, dark man with the deep, haunted eyes herself.

He didn't offer any conversation, but gave his full attention to his food. With his eyes focused on his plate, she took the opportunity to note the sinful length of his black lashes, the angular harshness of his jaw, the sensual fullness of his lower lip.

He looked up suddenly, his gaze locking with hers. The corner of his mouth curved upward in a mocking smile, letting her know he was aware of her intense perusal. She flushed and broke the connection, staring back down at her own plate.

What was wrong with her? Why was she so drawn to him? What was it about him that made her so physically aware of him? It had been nine long months since Jeffrey's death, and for the year before that the physical side of their marriage had been nonexistent. As always when she thought of Jeffrey, an arrow of guilt pierced through her and she consciously shoved away thoughts of him.

"Did you have a good day today?" she asked Forest, determined to have a normal conversation with the silent man.

He looked at her in surprise, as if her question was completely alien to him. "Yeah, fine." He hesitated a moment, then added. "What about you?"

"We explored the whole house. Don't worry, we steered clear of the basement," she replied.

"We found a really cool rocking horse in a room upstairs," Bobby blurted out.

"Bobby," Julie admonished her son. "Eat your green beans."

Bobby lowered his head, obviously disappointed at his mother's intervention in what had been most likely going to be an impassioned plea for the wooden horse.

The meal ended in silence, then Forest excused himself and disappeared. Julie sat waiting while Bobby finished eating.

"What that man needs is a wife and children of his own," Lottie observed as she cleared away Forest's plate. "He's lived here too long by himself."

"He's never been married?" Julie asked.

Lottie shook her head. "I've told him time and time again he should be filling this place with little children of his own. But he doesn't listen to me. Forest doesn't listen to anyone." She pressed her lips together, as if regretting what she'd said.

Julie had no problem believing that. Forest definitely seemed to be a man who lived by his own rules.

"Mom, I'm stuffed," Bobby said, patting his slender tummy with a contented sigh.

"Okay, you did a pretty good job cleaning your plate." For a moment Julie stared at her son, her mind whirling. She had to decide what they were going to do. If they were going to remain here, she needed to get him into school as soon as possible. Between packing and traveling, he'd missed a week of second grade. She didn't want him falling too far behind. Sometime this evening she needed to sit down and talk to Forest about her plans.

"What's the matter? What are you staring at? Do I have a glob of mashed potatoes on my nose or something?" Bobby asked, making Julie realize she'd been gazing intently at him.

"Nope, no mashed potatoes." She grinned at him. "I was just thinking that you look like a kid who needs a good beating at checkers."

"Ha, fat chance I'll take a beating!"

As mother and son scooted away from the table, Julie smiled at Lottie. "Thank you for a lovely dinner," she said.

Lottie waved her hands in dismissal. "Don't thank me. It's my job."

"Well, it was all delicious," Julie added, then she and Bobby went upstairs to their rooms. "You go get the checkerboard and we'll play in here on the floor," she said.

Bobby zoomed toward his bedroom, stopping in the doorway. "Wow!" he exclaimed.

Julie joined him there, shocked to see the wooden rocking horse standing in the corner by the window. Forest must have carried it down. "Why don't you get a damp washcloth from the bathroom so we can wipe the dust off him?"

"All right!" Bobby raced away in the direction of the bathroom. He returned a moment later with the requested washcloth. The game of checkers was forgotten as the two worked to clean the rich wood. Again Julie marveled at the workmanship of the piece, the exquisite attention to detail. Bobby's face flushed with excitement as he climbed up on the gleaming horse's back. As he rocked, the horse creaked rhythmically, a dull thump following each creak.

"Do I look like a cowboy?" Bobby asked.

Julie laughed. "Like a rootin' tootin' rodeo rider," she agreed, knowing that until the novelty wore off, the horse would be a big addition to Bobby's games of make-believe.

The evening passed quickly, consumed with a dozen games of checkers interspersed with Bobby "riding the range." By nine o'clock, the excitement of the day had worn out the little boy. Julie tucked him into bed, then went in search of Forest.

She found him in the living room, in the chair in front of the fire where he had sat the night before. For a moment she stood in the doorway, hesitant to disturb his obvious introspection. However, he must have sensed her presence. He turned and looked at her, his eyes momentarily revealing a pain beyond enduring, a torment too deep to bear. It was there only a moment, then gone, shuttered beneath a mocking smile. "Something you need?" he asked.

"I'd like to talk to you." She entered the room and sat in the chair across from him. "First of all, thank you . . . for letting Bobby use the horse."

He shrugged. "It was just sitting upstairs gathering dust." He focused his gaze back on the dancing flames in the stone fireplace. "It was made to be ridden."

"I appreciate your letting Bobby enjoy it." She sat for a moment. "I'm assuming you've resigned yourself to the fact that we're going to be here for a while?"

He looked at her darkly. "Do I have a choice?"

"No." She sighed and folded her hands together in her lap. "Forest, I know you don't want us here. But I have to be brutally honest." She felt a flush sweep into her cheeks. "We have nowhere else to go. We're broke, and we need to stay here long enough to get back on our feet."

"How long?" he asked.

She shrugged. "I don't know. A couple of months. We'd stay out of your way. Bobby would go to school, and I'll get a job. Within a couple of months we should be able to scrape together enough money to leave and start again someplace else."

"Jeffrey left you broke?" There was little surprise in Forest's voice. He shook his head and sighed ruefully. "Jeffrey never had a head for finances."

"We lived quite well. I had no idea what a horrible state our finances were in until his death. Jeffrey took care of those things—" Julie broke off, for a moment remembering the horror of having their home sold out from under them, their second car repossessed, even most of their furniture taken away by collectors who couldn't be paid. It had been a nightmare. "Bobby and I tried to hang on, but I realized all we had left was his inheritance here, and even that isn't worth anything as far as cash flow goes."

Forest leaned back in his chair and closed his eyes, one hand rising to rub his forehead. "You can't make us leave," Julie added with a touch of bravado. "We have a legal right to be here."

He opened his eyes and stared at her, his gaze moving slowly, insolently down the length of her. She felt the heat from his eyes and couldn't control the flush that warmed her cheeks. "You're right," he said. "I can't force you to leave. But I think you'll find Kingsdon Manor an inhospitable place."

"Certainly no more inhospitable than you are," she said with a touch of dry humor, perversely wanting to get a rise out of him, a flicker of emotion of any kind.

He laughed, showing a flash of pearl white teeth, and Julie felt her breath catch in her throat as she saw how attractive he looked with a genuine smile curving his lips. "I have a feeling with or without Kingsdon Manor you'd be fine."

"Probably, but Bobby needs to be here right now. He and Jeffrey were very close. He needs to see where his father grew up, needs this connection." Julie stared into the fire, remembering the horror of Jeffrey's death. There was a part of her that felt so guilty...guilty because in some small corner of her heart, his death had almost been a relief. Knowing how important it was for a boy to be with his father, she would have never divorced Jeffrey, even though their marriage wasn't an especially happy one. She'd believed in the sanctity of family and would have done nothing to break hers apart. Fate had done that for her.

"So, what kind of a job are you going to try to find?" Forest asked, pulling her from her painful thoughts.

She shrugged. "Whatever there is. I don't have many skills. I was in college when I met Jeffrey and he never wanted me to work."

"There aren't many opportunities for work in Kingsdon."

"I'll find something," she said with an assurance she didn't feel. She stared into the fire for a long moment, then looked at him curiously. "Jeffrey didn't talk much about his life here. He didn't talk much about you. What happened between the two of you?"

Again his mocking dark eyes swept over her. "I'll open up this house to you, Julie. But leave the past alone. What happened between me and my brother is really none of your business." He stood up. "Good night." Without a backward glance, he left her alone to the warmth of the fire and the questions that remained unanswered.

None of her business? He was wrong about that. The past that had shaped Jeffrey, caused his dark depressions and the emotional distance and disturbances that had made their marriage fall apart, was very much her business.

At least Forest seemed somewhat resigned to the fact that she and Bobby would be here for a while. First thing in the morning she would check into enrolling Bobby in the local school, then she would start the torturous task of job hunting.

She stifled a yawn with the back of one hand and decided to go to bed. Entertaining Bobby all day had taken its toll and a good night's sleep sounded blissful.

The minute she turned on the light in her bedroom, she heard the familiar creak and groan of the rocking horse. "Bobby," she said sharply as she strode across the room. "You should have been asleep an hour ago." She flipped on his light and stared at her son, sound asleep in his bed. In the corner by the window the rocking horse careened wildly back and forth, as if it were being ridden by a phantom cowboy.

CHAPTER THREE

"Come on, Bobby, you don't want to be late for your first day of school." Julie verbally prodded her son, who had been in his room for the past ten minutes, supposedly putting on his shoes. The early morning sunshine streaked in through the window, promising another beautiful day. Bobby giggled and said something too low for her to hear, then giggled again.

"Bobby?" Julie pulled the brush through her hair a final time, then went into the smaller room to see what her son found so entertaining. He sat cross-legged on the floor, looking at the empty chair next to the bed.

"Oh, it's cold in here. Do you have the window open?" He didn't answer for a moment. "Bobby?"

He started and smiled at her. "No, the window isn't open."

She looked at him curiously. "Are you ready to go?"

"I'm guess I'm ready." He stood up reluctantly, his smile gone.

Julie knew the emotions going through him and gave him a quick, reassuring hug. "You wait and see, it won't be so bad. You'll like the new school and you'll make lots of new friends today." She gave his thick hair a final combing with her fingertips. "Come on, we'd better go if we don't want you to be late."

"I don't care if I am," he replied.

"Well, I do," Julie answered. Before they left the room, she opened the curtains, hoping the sun shining in would chase away the chill.

Moments later they were in the car and driving toward Kingsdon Elementary School. As they entered the small community of Kingsdon, Julie looked around with interest.

It was a pleasant little town nestled against the foot of the hills. Brilliant autumn hues lent spectacular color to the tree-lined streets and manicured lawns. They passed the sawmill and advanced to Main Street.

Kingsdon's business district was laid out around the town square, a large park that had the county courthouse in the center. A sign at the entrance to the park announced the fall festival that weekend.

"Mom?" Bobby looked at her expectantly as she pulled up in front of the brick school building.

"What?" Julie parked the car and turned off the engine, then faced her son.

"Uncle Forest doesn't like me much, does he?"

Surprise winged through her at his words. "Oh, honey, I don't think it's that your uncle Forest doesn't like you..." She struggled for an explanation of Forest's distance, realizing she simply didn't have one, especially not one a little boy would understand. "Maybe it's just that he's not accustomed to having a kid around."

"I think he's sad," Bobby replied.

Again Julie was surprised. Sad? Perhaps. Certainly she'd caught a glimpse of deep shadows in Forest's eyes, shadows that seemed to radiate up from his heart, his soul. She shoved away thoughts of Forest and smiled at her son. "I'll tell you what would be sad . . . if we sat here in the car and talked for so long that you were late." She opened her door. "Come on, sport."

It took nearly half an hour to get Bobby squared away in his new second-grade class. She signed the papers that would allow his school in New York to transfer his records and discovered that, unlike the bus service in a bigger district, the school bus would, starting the next day, pick Bobby up and drop him off at his front door.

With him taken care of, Julie turned her energy to the task of job hunting. She drove back to the city square and found a parking place, then looked around, surveying the stores and offices that made up the business district.

She looked at her wristwatch, realizing it was still too early for most of the places to open. Instead of driving back up the hill to the house, she spied a café and decided to have a cup of coffee while she waited.

Pushing open the door to the café, she stepped inside and was instantly embraced by warm, moist air and the scent of cholesterol-laden cooking. It smelled wonderful. The pleasant smile on her lips wavered as she realized everyone in the place was looking at her. It was as if the whole scene in front of her was frozen, and the silence was deafening. She had the distinct feeling conversations had stopped midsentence the moment she'd walked in the door.

"Order up!" a voice yelled from the back, and that broke the curious spell, although Julie felt furtive glances directed at her as she slid onto a stool at the counter. She smiled uncertainly at a table of burly men who sat together toward the back of the café.

The waitress, a gray-haired, plump woman, approached her with a friendly smile. "Morning," she said as she handed Julie a menu.

"Good morning. Just coffee, please," Julie said, giving her back the menu.

The name tag the woman wore read Betty. "So, how you finding things up on the hill?" she asked as she poured the coffee.

"Fine," Julie replied, unable to hide her surprise.

Betty grinned. "We don't get many strangers in town. Heard Jeffrey's widow was staying up at Kingsdon Hill. I figure that's you."

Julie nodded, feeling the curious prickle on the back of her neck that told her she was still an object of interest for the others in the café. "I'm looking for a job. Do you know of anyone who needs any help?"

Betty leaned against the counter and shook her head. "Nope. Other than the mill, there aren't a whole lot of jobs to be had here."

"It seems like a nice little town."

Betty poured another cup of coffee. "It's all right, I suppose. We don't get a lot of new folks moving in. Most find us too small, too provincial, too gossipy for their liking."

She wiped a dribble of coffee from the pristine countertop. "I heard through the grapevine you've got a little boy."

Julie nodded. "Bobby. I just got him enrolled in the elementary school."

Betty leaned across the counter, so close that Julie could smell the rose scent of her perfume. "You keep an eye on that boy of yours, you hear?"

Something in her voice, a whispered urgency, caused Julie's heart to lurch in response. "What do you mean?"

"Betty?" A squat, chubby bald man stepped out from the kitchen area. "I'm not paying you to gossip, I'm paying you to work." He frowned at the waitress, then at Julie.

"You watch that boy of yours," Betty warned again, then carried the coffee to the table of men in the back.

Again an unnatural silence gripped the occupants of the café and as Julie heard the sound of the door swinging open, she turned to see Forest walking in. His eyes flared in surprise at the sight of her.

"Morning, Forest," Betty said as she set a mug on the counter next to where Julie sat.

"Betty," he returned, and he nodded at the men at the back table. Julie was acutely aware of him as he eased himself onto the counter stool next to hers. He usurped all the space, his firmly muscled leg pressing warmly against her own.

His scent surrounded her—the wild smell of timber, the clean scent of fresh wood shavings and sawdust. It was a pleasant, intensely masculine smell, one she found extremely attractive.

She wanted to move her leg away from his, but didn't want him to think he made her uncomfortable. Besides, she didn't find the intimate contact uncomfortable, she found it decidedly provocative.

She hadn't seen him that morning. He'd left before she and Bobby had gone down to breakfast. She now turned to him, as always noting the aura of darkness that seemed to cling to him no matter what he wore, no matter what his expression. "You come here often?" she asked, more to begin a conversation than for any other reason.

"Every morning for my coffee break." His large hands curled around his coffee cup. He fixed his gaze on it, as if ignoring her would make her go away.

"I decided to come in for a quick cup of coffee before I start job hunting." She willed him to look at her, converse with her. "You are the most taciturn man I think I've ever met," she finally exclaimed irritably. "You can't even make a stab at the pretense of sociable conversation."

He turned on his stool, the movement causing his leg to press more forcefully again her own. He eyed her, his dark brows raised mockingly. "Nice weather we're having, isn't it?"

"Yes, it is," she answered easily, as if she didn't notice the sarcasm in his voice and didn't want to wring his thickly muscled neck. "I hope it stays nice for the fall festival this weekend."

"It's supposed to rain," he said, turning back and staring into his cup.

"Ah well, a little rain won't keep Bobby and me away. I'm anxious to meet all the people Jeffrey grew up with and learn a little about his past." She wanted to say that she sensed secrets here—secrets about Jeffrey and what had driven him away from Kingsdon Hill. She'd sensed secrets in Lottie's eyes, too, and again in Betty's strange words.

If possible, Forest's countenance darkened, but he didn't say anything. Instead he turned on his stool and nodded again to the men at the table in the back.

"I'm fixing twelve of my famous rhubarb pies for the festival," Betty said.

"Rhubarb pie. That sounds wonderful," Julie observed.

"You ain't tasted *Betty's* rhubarb pie," a burly man at the back table replied teasingly.

Betty snorted. "It wasn't leafy salads that gave you that belly." The rest of the men laughed, but it was a hollow sound.

Julie looked at her wristwatch, oddly relieved to realize it was time for her to start hitting the business establishments. Something wasn't right here, and she had no idea what it was. There was tension in the air, a palpable tension that seemed to radiate from Betty, from the men at the table and most especially from Forest.

Murmuring a quick goodbye to Betty, then nodding to Forest, she put a dollar on the counter and left the café.

She'd gone only a few steps when her arm was grabbed from behind. She whirled around to see Forest. "What are you doing?" she asked, jerking her arm from his grasp.

"I want to talk to you."

"So talk," she replied, chilled despite the warmth of the sunshine overhead.

"The festival is supposed to be a day of fun. It's a day to visit with neighbors, laugh with co-workers." His eyes narrowed as they bore into hers. "It's not a day to dig into the past." In the black of his eyes she saw the spectral presence of inner demons, the forlorn darkness of hell. "Just leave it alone, Julie." His voice was slightly hoarse with suppressed emotion. "Jeffrey is dead and nothing can be served by rooting around in what happened long ago. Just leave it the hell alone."

"What are you so afraid of?" Julie asked softly.

His face blanched and for a moment she was afraid she'd gone too far. "I'm not afraid of anything but mouthy women asking too many questions, digging into business that has nothing to do with them." He turned and strode away from her as she stared wordlessly after him. When he had turned out of sight, the sun suddenly seemed brighter, warmer. She frowned thoughtfully. There were secrets here, secrets that for some reason Forest didn't want discovered. What had happened in the past that he didn't want her to know?

Despite her feeling that Bobby needed to be here, had seemed to react positively to these new surroundings, Julie couldn't help but feel that the best thing she could do for all of them was get together some money and get the hell away from Kingsdon Hill.

* * *

"Oh boy, this looks like fun!" Bobby exclaimed as he and Julie walked through the entrance to the town park. On a bandstand in front of the courthouse musicians played a raucous rendition of a Sousa march, and the air was redolent with the smoky scent of barbecue. There was a festive excitement in the air as throngs of people milled around, obviously enjoying the mild autumn weather. The rain that Forest had predicted hadn't materialized, and it was a perfect day for outdoor activities.

"There's Jimmy." Bobby pointed to a young boy standing near the barbecue pit. "Hey, Jimmy!" he yelled, then he looked at his mother in silent appeal.

"Go on," she said, and smiled as he immediately shot off to join his little friend. She moved over to a picnic bench near a huge oak tree and sat down, enjoying the warmth of the sun on her back. She watched as Bobby and Jimmy giggled and shoved each other in the eternal bonding process of young males.

Bobby had settled into school with surprising ease. He liked his teacher, Mrs. Watkins, who he said smelled like roses and always talked nice. The week of school he had missed while they traveled didn't seem to have put him behind, and he'd even managed to make half a dozen new friends. Bobby's relatively easy adjustment was about all that was perfect with her life at the moment.

Julie had spent the last week job hunting to no avail. Each day she'd come back to the house a little more dispirited than when she'd left. If she didn't know better she would swear it was a conspiracy and everyone had been warned not to give her a job. She sighed. She'd been in Kingsdon a week and still had no prospects. Nor was she any closer to a relationship with her husband's brother than she'd been when she'd lived a thousand miles away.

As thoughts of Forest entered her mind, she looked around, knowing that he'd left the house early that morning to help ready things for the festival. She spotted him standing beneath a large tree, the colored leaves above him casting shadows on his face and shoulders.

He stood alone, surveying the crowd like a despot overlooking his empire. As always, he was dressed informally, in a checkered flannel shirt that stretched across the broadness of his chest, and a pair of jeans that had long ago conformed to the muscled contours of his buttocks and legs. He looked primitive, like a frontiersman come to town to spend his hard-earned money on women and whiskey.

There was something about the man that hit her in an intensely physical way. He'd been rude, almost threatening toward her since the moment she'd arrived at his house, but that didn't dispel her fascination with him. She'd seen very little of him through the last week, consciously staying out of his way. However, whenever they had encountered each other the tension rippled between them, a tension that made it difficult for her to draw a full breath when in his presence.

Why hadn't he married? He should be considered the catch of the town. He was relatively wealthy, single and attractive...and he had dark shadows in his eyes that proclaimed loudly Do Not Trespass. Julie sighed, realizing she'd answered her own question of why he wasn't married. He didn't invite closeness from anyone. It was like he kept an invisible shield around himself to keep others away. What she couldn't figure out was why she felt so compelled to breach that shield and draw to the surface the obscure secrets she sensed he held within.

It was obvious that something horrible had happened between Forest and Jeffrey, something causing a deep turmoil that still affected Forest. He refused to talk about Jeffrey, refused to give her any clue as to what had happened between the two brothers. She had a feeling that if she could solve that particular mystery, she would be much closer to understanding the severe depressions that had assaulted Jeffrey, the nightmares that had often caused him to weep in his sleep.

She felt her breath tightening in her chest as he sauntered toward her. As always when his eyes played over her, she had the disturbing impression that he could see through her clothing. She felt naked and vulnerable beneath the heat of his gaze. She was also aware of other people watching them, as if expecting some sort of high drama.

"Afternoon, Julie," he said, his voice mockingly pleasant.

"Good afternoon, Forest. It's a beautiful day for the festival, isn't it?"

He nodded, dark amusement darting in his eyes. "Why is it we seem to always discuss the weather?"

She shrugged. "I was just making an idle observation." She cast a furtive look around and noted again that she and Forest held the attention of the people around them. "Why is everyone looking at us?" she asked.

Forest looked around in turn, his amusement more obvious now as it curled the corners of his lips. "This is a small town, Julie. A small town that thrives on gossip. I'm the boss man, the king of the castle, so to speak." His dark eyes drew her in, and without conscious thought she leaned closer to him. "You know what they'll be saying?" He reached out and touched a strand of her hair, his touch sending shock waves through her. "They'll say we're lovers."

She gasped and stepped back. "That's ridiculous," she scoffed.

"Idle gossip usually is." He hesitated a moment, as if he wanted to say more. Then his eyes darkened, and with a curt nod he moved away and left her standing alone.

"He's a handsome hunk, isn't he?"

Julie jumped at the sound of the friendly voice coming from just behind her. She turned to see an attractive, ash blond woman grinning at her knowingly. "I'm Lorna Richards, ace reporter, editor and owner of the *Kingsdon Gazette*."

"Hi, I'm Julie Kingsdon."

"Oh, I know who you are...the gossip mill in this community is the most healthy thing about it." She grinned candidly, displaying a chipped front tooth that only added to her charm. "I know you have a little boy who started school this past week, and I know you've been pounding the pavement looking for a job. Any luck?''

Julie shook her head. "I think I've knocked on every door of every establishment in this town, and nobody needs any help."

"You didn't knock on mine."

Julie smiled at Lorna. "You're right. But I'm fairly unskilled and definitely don't have a degree in journalism. I figured it would be a waste of your time and mine."

"Can you type? Answer a phone?"

"Well, sure, but—"

"Then you're hired. You can start Monday morning." Lorna laughed at Julie's expression of surprise. "My secretary quit two weeks ago because she had a baby."

"But I don't know anything about reporting or newspapers," Julie protested.

"You don't have to. I do all that stuff. I just need somebody to be my girl Friday." She held out her hand to Julie. "Deal?"

"Deal." Julie shook her hand, feeling a renewed burst of optimism. She had no idea what Lorna intended to pay her, had no idea what hours she would work or exactly what she would do, but it didn't matter. She'd taken the first step in getting on with her life.

"Now, let's get to the good stuff...the gossip." Lorna grinned irreverently. "How are you finding things up on the hill?"

Julie looked over at Forest. "Rather chilly. I showed up uninvited, and Forest hasn't been thrilled," she answered, then bit her tongue. After all, she was speaking to a reporter.

Lorna laughed, then sobered as she nodded her head toward the tall man. "I can imagine. He's always been sort of a loner with a chip on his shoulder."

Julie turned to Lorna with interest. "You've known him a long time?"

"He's the one who chipped my tooth when we were in junior high school. We all went to school together, and my parents were friends with Richard Kingsdon. I was two years older than Forest and several years younger than Jeffrey. We were at their house visiting and a fight broke out between the two boys. Forest went to hit Jeffrey with a tin can and got me instead. By the way, I was sorry to hear about Jeffrey's death."

Julie nodded, then looked back to where Forest was now standing, near the barbecue pit. "So the two brothers weren't close?"

"Half brothers," Lorna replied, and Julie turned to her in shock. She winced. "You didn't know that Jeffrey and Forest were half brothers?"

"No, I had no idea."

"Jeffrey's mother died when he was two, after a long illness. The speculation is that Forest was the product of a brief fling Richard had with a woman who worked as his secretary for a couple of years. When Forest was born, she left town, and nobody knows what happened to her."

Julie silently digested this new information. "Jeffrey rarely spoke of Forest, but when he did he never mentioned Forest being a half brother."

"That's odd. He loved to torment Forest when they were younger."

Julie looked at Lorna curiously. Finally...finally she was getting some answers. "Torment how?"

"Oh, you know...hateful kid stuff, like throwing it in Forest's face that his mother didn't want him and that his birth was just an unfortunate accident. Jeffrey could be pretty mean, and Forest would take it for so long, then he'd have a fearsome explosion of anger." Lorna's face colored slightly. "Sorry, I shouldn't be talking ill of the dead, and Jeffrey was your husband."

Julie smiled. "He was my husband, but I'm aware he wasn't a saint." She had occasionally seen glimpses of Jeffrey's cruelty in the years they had been married.

"No man I've ever known was a saint." Lorna shook her head and laughed ruefully. "Me, I've been married and divorced three times, and believe me, none of them were saints." She grinned saucily. "I've got the getting-married part down pat...it's staying married that gives me trouble."

Julie laughed, feeling an instant liking for the woman.

"Come on," Lorna said suddenly. "Let's go get a cold beer."

Julie looked around for Bobby and found him playing on the jungle gym with a number of other boys. Seeing that he was occupied and having fun, she nodded to Lorna and stood up. Together the two of them walked over to where beer kegs were set up.

"Two, Charlie," Lorna said to the man working the keg.

"Coming right up." He filled two plastic glasses with the foamy brew and handed them to the women. "You're looking mighty fine today, Lorna," he said with a flirtatious grin.

"So's your wife, Charlie Maxwell, and she's bigger and meaner than both of us, so you'd do well to watch yourself." Lorna laughed as the big man looked sheepish. "Let's go over there in the shade." She pointed to another picnic table near the playground equipment where Bobby was playing.

Once the two were settled at the table, Julie took a sip of the cold beer. "It's been years since I've had a beer," she said. "Jeffrey wasn't much of a drinker, even socially."

"He never did much drinking when he was younger, either. Now Forest, he was a horse of a different color. When he was a teenager he was a real wild child."

Julie looked to where Forest now stood with a small group of men. He was speaking and his face was lit with an animation she hadn't seen before. Again she felt a curious pull toward him, an attraction stronger than anything she'd ever felt before. She looked back at Lorna, disturbed by her own emotions where Forest was concerned.

"You've got a cute kid," Lorna observed.

Julie smiled. "Thanks. He's a good kid, but he really misses his daddy."

"It's tough to lose a parent when you're so young." Lorna shook her head sadly. "It's tough to lose anyone you love. But time heals some of the hurt. A lot of people in this town thought Jeffrey would never marry again after he lost his first wife.''

"His first wife?" Julie stared at Lorna in confusion. "What do you mean?"

This time it was Lorna's turn to look at Julie incredulously. "You didn't know that Jeffrey had been married before?" Julie shook her head, for a moment feeling like she'd been punched in the stomach. Lorna sighed and withdrew a pack of cigarettes from her purse. "Wow, I had no idea you didn't know." She lit a cigarette and inhaled deeply. "If smoking doesn't kill me one of these days, my big mouth will." She looked back at Julie. "I suppose if you don't know about his first wife, then you don't know about his son, either."

"His son?" The words choked in Julie's throat, and for a moment she felt like she was swimming in a sea of unreality. "Jeffrey had a son?" She thought of Bobby. Did he have a half brother running around somewhere in the town of Kingsdon? *Oh, Jeffrey, what does all this mean? Why didn't you tell me?* What else didn't she know about the man she had been married to for eight years? "Where…do they live here in Kingsdon?" she finally managed to ask, through the constriction of her throat.

Lorna shook her head. "His wife, MaryAnn, died from complications right after childbirth. Jeffrey hardly had time to mourn her, what with a newborn to care for. Those three Kingsdon men doted on that baby. Little Christopher ruled that roost, and a special bond seemed to develop between Forest and the little fellow.''

"So what happened? Where is Christopher now?" A curious sense of dread accompanied Julie's question.

"He's, uh, dead."

"Oh, how sad. What happened to him?" Julie asked, trying to fight her way through a myriad of emotions.

Lorna looked over at Forest, who now appeared to be watching them. She compressed her lips tightly. "Look, I've said far more than I should have.'' Nervously she ran a hand through her short blond hair.

"You can't stop now," Julie protested. Her head spun dizzily with the information she'd received. "What happened to Christopher? How did he die?"

Again Lorna shot a look at Forest. Julie followed her gaze. His eyes suddenly met hers, a heated glimpse that whispered of suppressed anger, dark secrets and haunting guilt. For a moment time seemed suspended and she felt herself falling into the black hole of his gaze, falling into an abyss so devoid of life, so devoid of love that it frightened her. She averted her head, breaking the visual contact with him as she looked back at Lorna.

"Lorna, please. Tell me what happened to Christopher." Julie continued pressing, her need to know exploding inside her. She reached out and grabbed the reporter's hand in hers. It was cold, lifeless, and she suddenly realized Lorna was afraid. "Tell me," she whispered urgently.

Lorna shook her head and gently freed her hand from Julie's grasp. "If you really want to know what happened to little Christopher...ask Forest."

Julie looked back at Forest. Despite the distance that separated them, she could feel his tension, see the darkness of his eyes. Suddenly she, too, was afraid.

CHAPTER FOUR

Darkness filled the bedroom. The moon was hidden behind black clouds that had moved in near dusk. Bobby lay on his back in bed, knowing he should be asleep, but sleep was the farthest thing from his mind.

It had been an awesome day...the best that he could remember in a long time. He'd watched a log-splitting contest and had run in a three-legged race with Jimmy as his partner. They hadn't won, but they'd laughed so hard Bobby's tummy still hurt.

Of course, his tummy might hurt because he'd eaten three hot dogs, a bunch of spicy ribs, two cotton candies and a big plate of beans. He and Jimmy had also shared a glass of beer, which Jimmy had managed to sneak from one of the kegs. Bobby was glad his mom hadn't found out about the beer. She would have had a fit, and that would have made his tummy hurt even more. Besides, he hadn't liked it very much, although he had told Jimmy it tasted great.

He turned over on his side, staring out the window into the darkness of the night. The wind had picked up and tree branches scratched against the windowpane. He pulled the blanket closer around him. The branches sounded kind of creepy.

He missed his daddy. There had been times when his dad hadn't been nice, when he'd screamed and yelled, then cried. Those times had scared Bobby. But then there had been times when his dad had cuddled him close and held him so tightly it had stolen his breath. It had felt good. Missing his dad was a hurt inside him that never went away. He felt it now, stabbing in his heart, causing tears to burn in his eyes. He wiped them away, refusing to be a baby and give in to them.

He wished his uncle Forest was nicer. There were times when he looked at him and Bobby had the feeling he wanted to be friends. But then there were other times when his uncle Forest's eyes scared him. He shivered, thinking of when his uncle stared at him and looked mean.

A whisper of cold air suddenly sailed over him, cold enough to penetrate the blanket he was under. A faint, boyish giggle followed. Bobby rolled over and sat up, peering into the inky darkness of his room with excitement. "Hi. Where are you?"

Another soft giggle filled the room, first coming from the rocking horse, then from the opposite direction. Bobby smiled, knowing his new friend was playing games. He waited impatiently, his gaze skittering around the dark room. Then he saw him. A faint glow appeared, a glow in the form of a small figure sitting on the back of the rocking horse. As Bobby watched, the glow grew dimmer and the figure took a more solid form. He was about Bobby's age, and dark-haired like him. He was dressed the same as he'd been the last time Bobby had seen him, in a pair of worn jeans and a bright red sweatshirt.

"I wondered if you'd come back to see me again," Bobby said softly.

I'm back. He didn't speak aloud, but rather talked in Bobby's head. It was as clear to Bobby as if he said the words out loud.

"How do you do that?" he whispered.

How do I do what?

"How do you talk in my head?"

The little boy grinned. *I just do it,* he replied. *I can do lots of things.*

"Like what?" Bobby pulled his legs up against his chest and wrapped his arms around them, enthralled with his new companion.

I can fly.

"Show me," Bobby replied. He gasped and clapped his hands in glee as his friend floated up above the rocking horse, then moved to hover directly above where Bobby sat on his bed. He laughed as his friend floated down to sit next to him on the mattress.

"Bobby?" At the sound of his mother's voice, Bobby's friend vanished.

Julie turned on the bedroom light and frowned at her son. "You're supposed to be asleep. What are you doing in here?"

"I was talking to my new friend, but he disappeared when you came in."

"A new friend?" Julie entered the room, immediately shivering as a draft of icy air enveloped her. "Why is this room so cold? Do you have the window open?" She looked toward the closed window, then checked to make certain the heat vent was open.

Maybe she should speak to Forest about the drafts in this room.

Sitting on the edge of Bobby's bed, she pulled the blankets up tightly around his neck. "Now, what's this about a new friend?"

"I don't know his name, but he's come to visit me twice."

"And he disappeared when I came in here?" Julie asked, and Bobby nodded. An imaginary friend. For some reason this new development didn't particularly worry her. Bobby had always been an imaginative child, and when he was five he'd had a make-believe friend named Gifford who he insisted was a furry rabbit. Every night for a month Gifford had eaten dinner with them and had slept with Bobby. Then, as mysteriously as he'd appeared, Gifford had vanished.

With Jeffrey's death still so painful to Bobby, Julie wasn't surprised that a new fanciful friend had come into her son's life. "And is your new friend a bunny rabbit, or a fat, ugly toad?" she teased.

Bobby looked at her with disgust and rolled his eyes. "Mom, he's not an animal. He's a little boy like me, and he can fly all around the room. He makes me laugh."

Julie lightly touched the end of his nose. "That's the best kind of friend to have, the kind who makes you laugh." She smoothed his hair away from his forehead, then kissed him soundly. "But I don't like new friends who keep my son up past his bedtime, and your bedtime was long ago." She gave him a final smile. "Now go to sleep."

She blew him a kiss from the doorway, then shut off the light and left the room. She went through her own bedroom and down the stairs. Ever since she and Bobby had come home from the festival earlier in the evening, she'd been waiting for Forest to return. She wanted to talk to him about Christopher. She needed to talk to him.

After she'd spoken to Lorna, the rest of the day had passed in a haze for Julie. The woman's words had whirled around and around in her head, creating a dizzying affect she couldn't seem to shake off. She'd met a hundred people during the afternoon, but she couldn't remember a single name... except the name Christopher.

She curled up on the sofa, grateful that Lottie had built a fire before she'd left the house for the night. The warmth radiated outward and comforted her. She'd been cold all day, enclosed in a chill of half madness as she realized her relationship with Jeffrey had been built on lies of omission.

How could he have not told her about his first wife? His child? How could he have kept such an important piece of himself, his past, a secret? It was no wonder they had never achieved the kind of closeness she'd longed for, needed; he'd kept a large portion of himself private and unattainable.

She jumped as a flash of lightning flickered outside the window, followed by a low rumble of thunder a moment later. Oh, good, she thought irritably. A storm seemed a perfect ending to an emotionally tumultuous day.

She'd thought the darkness of night would bring Forest home, but it had been dark for nearly two hours, and he hadn't returned. Surely if it began to rain, he would come back.

She didn't know how long the festival would last, didn't know if it was still going on. If it was, surely the rain would put an abrupt end to the festivities.

Julie was aware of the wind picking up, slapping tree limbs against the windows in the living room, creating a mournful whistle as it blew around the corners of the huge house. Above its siren call, the low sound of sobbing drifted to her.

She sat up, tilting her head with a frown, unsure if it was somehow connected to the wind or something entirely different. It rose and fell, and she finally recognized it as the eerie, pitiful sobbing of a child.

She jumped up and headed for the stairs. Bobby had always been afraid of storms. He'd always been afraid of thunder. She turned on the light that lit the stairwell, then climbed upward, pausing midway as the electricity flickered off, then came back on. She continued her ascent, anxious to get to Bobby and ease his fear. When she got to her room, she moved through the darkness and stood in the doorway that led to Bobby's smaller room. She could hear his breathing...the deep, regular rhythm of sleep. Above that, the crying persisted. A flash of lightning revealed Bobby in his bed, sound asleep.

Julie's mouth suddenly went dry and her breathing grew shallow with fear. Calm down, she told herself as she retraced her steps back to the hallway. Lightning slashed the sky again, spilling erratic light into the long hall. Thunder rumbled closer and the crying seemed to intensify in volume. Cold chills danced up her arms, then down her spine in response to the childlike weeping.

The house suddenly felt cold around her, unnaturally cold. She hesitated, the haunting noise louder now, as if she were closer to the source. She followed it down the hallway, past Forest's bedroom, past the spare rooms and the second bath. Then it stopped. Julie could hear the moaning of the wind, but the weeping stopped as suddenly as it had started.

She stood unmoving at the end of the hallway, her heart pounding with abnormal rapidity. Had it been real? Had the sound of a child crying been genuine or had she imagined it? God knew, her mind was filled with thoughts that would be conducive to imagining something like this. All day long her head had been full of old mysteries, haunting secrets and the mysterious death of a poor little boy. It wouldn't surprise her to discover the crying had been part of her overly active imagination.

She started back down the stairs, stifling a scream as the electricity once again flickered off...on...then it stayed off. She stood still in the middle of the stairs, waiting for the light to come back on. After several moments she realized the storm had intensified outside and the electricity might remain off indefinitely.

Grabbing the banister, blinded by the profound darkness, she eased her way down the remaining steps. When she reached the bottom, she bumped headfirst into a solid wall of flesh. A scream rose to her throat and spilled out of her. She started to fall backward, but her shoulders were grabbed by large hands.

"What the hell are you doing running around in the dark?" Forest demanded.

"I didn't start running around in the dark. I was halfway down the stairs when the lights went off." She shrugged away from him and bumped into the ornate umbrella stand, which she couldn't see. She stifled a protest as he grasped her arm and led her out of the darkness to the living room, where the fire provided reassuring illumination. "I didn't know you were home," she said as she breathed a sigh of relief and sat down on the sofa.

"I've been here for hours. I've been downstairs in my workroom." He eased himself into the chair she had begun to think of as his. It was the huge wing chair closest to the fire. She'd never seen him sit anyplace else in the room.

"What do you do down there?" Julie asked curiously.

His gaze was dark and enigmatic. "Whatever I want to do."

Julie nodded, trying to figure out the best way to broach the subject she most wanted to talk about. "I have a job," she said, deciding to talk about the easy things first.

His dark eyebrows rose curiously. "Where?"

"At the newspaper. I'm going to be Lorna Richards's girl Friday."

A flicker of humor danced in the darkness of his eyes, and the corner of his lips curved upward. "You'll find Lorna colorful, to say the least."

"She seems very nice."

"Oh, she is. Lorna is a jewel to everyone but the man who finds himself her husband." A genuine smile lit his features. "Lorna has a tendency to suck the lifeblood out of her husbands."

Julie smiled, easily able to see Lorna doing that. "I'm just grateful she's giving me a chance at a job." She hesitated, wanting to speak to Forest about Jeffrey's first wife, his little boy. She wanted to find out what had happened to Christopher. But she was reluctant to bring up a topic she knew would make him angry.

For the first time since she'd arrived, Forest appeared relatively at ease. The lines on his face were relaxed and the tension that usually radiated from him was gone. For the first time he seemed open, less guarded, and she didn't want to do or say anything to disturb the tenuous peace of the moment.

"Everyone seemed to have a good time today," she observed.

He nodded. "I started the fall festivals ten years ago as a way to bring together the community and thank the people who work for me at the mill. I tried it the first year, and it was such a rousing success, I decided it should be an annual town event."

Lightning slashed the semidarkness of the room and a clap of thunder sounded directly overhead. "It's a good thing the storm held off until now," Julie observed. "How long do you think the electricity will be off?"

"Who knows? It almost always goes out when we have a storm." He stood up and put another log on the fire. Squatting on his haunches, he took the poker and jabbed at the wood on the grate, a shower of sparks engulfing the new piece. He put the poker back, then stood up and looked at her. "I think I'll call it a night. It's been a long day." He headed toward the doorway.

"Forest . . . wait. I need to talk to you." Julie stood up, knowing that if she wanted some answers, she needed to ask questions now. He turned and looked at her curiously. "I know about Jeffrey's first wife. I know about Christopher."

The name hung in the air between them. Forest's mouth compressed into a tight line and his eyes blackened with suppressed emotions. "If you know all about it, then you don't need to talk to me."

"I don't know everything, and I do need to talk to you," she protested, moving to stand directly in front of him. "I have to know what happened. You might claim the past as belonging only to you, but that's not true. Whatever happened years ago had a significant affect on my life as well."

"What are you talking about?" he asked, his sentence punctuated by another clap of thunder.

"I married a man who suffered deep depressions, a man who was incapable of achieving the kind of emotional intimacy I wanted and needed." Tears burned in Julie's eyes, tears of regret, guilt and a deep sorrow she knew would follow her for years to come. "Whatever happened had a profound affect on Jeffrey, and that had an equally profound affect on my life. I need to know what happened."

His eyes were cold, emotionless. "You've had a week to ask your questions around town, hear all the rumors about what happened to Christopher."

"Nobody has told me anything. It's like everyone is afraid to talk about it. I know Christopher is dead, but I don't want to listen to rumors. I want the truth. Lorna told me that if I want to know what happened to Christopher, I should ask you." She held his gaze, not flinching beneath the fiery anger that burned there.

He seemed to grow with his rage. His shoulders expanded as he drew in a deep breath. "What makes you so certain I'll tell you the truth?"

She shrugged. "I guess I'll just have to trust you."

He laughed, a harsh, bitter sound that echoed the thunder rumbling overhead. "Trusting me would be your first mistake." Beneath the rancor of his words was an ache of anguish that pierced through her. She suddenly realized that whatever had happened, it had left an indelible mark on this man, a scar every bit as deep as the one left on Jeffrey. She also realized his rage masked pain, an enormous pain of such proportion it momentarily stole her breath away.

"Trusting you is all I have," she finally said softly. She reached out and took one of his hands, marveling at the warmth of his flesh against her own chilled skin. He tried for a moment to yank away, then with a deep sigh allowed her to lead him over to the sofa. She sat down next to him, intensely aware of the heat of his body so close to hers.

"Please, tell me what happened. Tell me about Christopher." She gently squeezed his hand, then released it, uncomfortable by the warmth the physical contact provoked inside her.

Forest winced, as if hearing the child's name was physically painful. He leaned forward and buried his face in his hands, the firelight etching him in golden tones that did nothing to soften his obvious agony.

When he finally lifted his head, his eyes were still filled with torment. "I can't," he said faintly.

"You have to," Julie persisted. "If you can't talk about it for yourself, then do it for me. I have to know what happened to him."

He leaned back in the chair and released a weary sigh of resignation, his fight unexpectedly gone. "Christopher was the brightest, most loving child I've ever known." His voice was low, so soft she had to lean forward to hear him. "From the moment he was a toddler, he loved me as nobody else had in my entire life—unconditionally, eternally, absolutely. He greeted me every day with a good-morning kiss and insisted I be the one who tucked him in each night." He closed his eyes for a moment, as if savoring those precious memories from the past.

He opened his eyes and looked at Julie curiously. "Jeffrey never said anything to you about MaryAnn or Christopher?"

"Nothing." This time Julie heard the hollowness in her own voice as she realized Jeffrey's refusal to talk about his past was indicative of all that had been wrong with their marriage. "I always sensed there was something in his past...something that had hurt him, scarred him."

"Hatred. That's what did it. The kind of hatred that twists in your guts and tears out your heart." Again his voice was soft, and she could see his own grief weighing heavily in the slump of his shoulders, the weary expression on his face.

She leaned closer to him, wanting to wrap her arms around him and ease the shadows from his eyes, assuage the pain that radiated from him as strongly as his prominent, masculine scent. "Tell me," she urged softly. "Tell me what happened to Christopher."

"It was a long time ago. I don't remember all the specifics." He drew himself up defensively. Outside, the storm seemed to reach its zenith, creating a spastic light show complete with thunderous booms.

Julie studied his features, so handsome, yet so racked with a soul-deep affliction. "I know he's dead. How did he die? An accident?"

He stared into the fire, as if lost for a moment in the blazing flame. Time seemed suspended as Julie waited for him to speak. "It happened a couple weeks after the accident at the mill that killed my father. I was injured in the same accident, hit in the temple with a load of wood." His voice was flat, as if he'd successfully removed himself emotionally from the painful events. "I'd been off work recuperating, and during the days I baby-sat Christopher, while Jeffrey went to the mill." His voice was hoarse, as if the mere act of remembering stole most of his breath. "I remember giving him cereal for breakfast. He was mad because he wanted me to fix him pancakes, and I didn't want the mess."

A winsome smile suddenly crossed his features and Julie drew her own breath in sharply at the beauty it brought to his face. "Christopher was more than a little spoiled. He threw temper tantrums when he didn't get his way. He had one that morning, stamping his feet and telling me he hated me." His voice caught in his throat and he looked up at her, his dark eyes liquid with unshed tears. "I should have let him have his way that morning. I should have made him pancakes. I should have given him anything he wanted."

This time Julie didn't fight her impulse. She reached out again and took his hand. For a moment it remained slack, then he curled his fingers through hers, gripping tightly. "We spent the morning playing hide-and-seek," he continued. "Christopher loved to play that game." His voice was tense, as if his throat had constricted. "After lunch I insisted we have some quiet time. I sat right here and Christopher stretched out in front of the fire on the floor."

Forest dropped her hand and stood up. When he turned back to face her, his eyes reflected the red of the fire's glow, an unearthly light of damnation. "I fell asleep." He whispered the words, as if he'd just confessed to a mortal sin. "I fell asleep, and when I woke up I was standing in the middle of the forest and Christopher was gone."

Julie frowned, unable to comprehend exactly what he was saying. "You were asleep and he just disappeared? I don't understand."

He drew himself up, and it was as if the storm had moved inside, into the room ... into him. Tension vibrated in the air and a clap of thunder caused Julie to jump half out of her seat.

Forest rubbed a hand over his face, and when he looked back at her, his features again displayed anger. "You shouldn't have made me go through this all over again. I don't know what happened to Christopher. Damn it, I don't know." The rage slowly left his face and he gazed at her coldly, dispassionately. "But I can tell you what Jeffrey thought happened."

"And what's that?" she asked.

He hesitated a moment, his eyes not leaving hers. "Jeffrey thought I killed Christopher. He thought I took him out in the woods and killed him, then buried the body where nobody would ever find it. To this day it hasn't been found."

Julie's heart thumped in an unsteady rhythm and for a moment she was sorry she'd asked, sorry she'd pried. She'd had no idea it was such an ugly past. "And what do you think happened?" she asked in a subdued whisper.

Again the light of the damned shone from his eyes and his mouth twisted in a bitter smile. "I think the same thing, Julie. I think I took that little boy out into the woods and killed him."

CHAPTER FIVE

Julie stared at him, unsure what to believe, what to think. His words pulsated in the air, as if with a life force and energy of their own.

Forest slumped back in the chair, his internal storm apparently spent with the confession.

"I . . . I don't understand. If you killed Christopher, then why aren't you in jail?" she finally asked incredulously. She sank down on the sofa again and continued to stare at him. "Surely there was some sort of an investigation?"

Forest laughed bitterly, the weathered lines of his face deepening. "If that's what you want to call it. Sheriff Wolvertine asked me some questions, then released me."

"If the sheriff thought you were responsible for Christopher's disappearance, he would have arrested you," she protested. Nothing made sense, especially his confession of sorts. Why would Forest kill a child he'd obviously loved with all his heart? And how was it possible to kill somebody while you slept? It made no sense. Nothing made sense.

"Hell, Sheriff Wolvertine wasn't about to arrest me for anything," Forest scoffed. "He's got three sons who work for me at the mill, as do most of the men in this town. Families depend on the mill—this whole town depends on it. With me in prison and Jeffrey on the verge of an emotional breakdown, the whole operation would have folded, and all those men would have lost their livelihoods.''

''If he'd thought you were guilty, he wouldn't have let you go,'' Julie repeated firmly.

Forest stared at her long and hard. ''Are you really that naive, or just a damned fool?''

Julie flushed and raised her chin a notch. ''I guess I'm just a damned fool, because none of this makes any kind of sense to me. You say that you don't know what happened between the time you went to sleep and the moment you woke up in the woods, and yet you're so certain you killed Christopher. Why?''

Forest's look was baleful, and a tic moved erratically in the lean muscle under his cheekbone. ''That's what I said.'' He raked a hand through his hair, his features creased in aggravation. ''Look, I went through all this ten years ago, and I don't intend to rehash it now. It's done, it's over and nothing can ever change what happened that day.'' He stood up once again, and there was a sardonic lift to his sooty eyebrows. ''You wanted to know all the deep, dark secrets of the past. Well, now you know them.'' He turned, obviously intending to leave the room.

''Forest...wait.'' Julie jumped up out of her chair, still feeling that the tragedy remained as much a puzzle as ever. She couldn't leave it at this, with so many questions still whirling around in her head, so many pieces not fitting together. ''How do you know Christopher is dead? If his body was never found, then how

do you know he wasn't kidnapped, taken by somebody?''

Again his shoulders slumped and despair washed
over his features. He suddenly looked achingly young,
devoid of hope, vulnerable as a child who found himself alone and abandoned. "I know he's dead. I knew
it the moment I woke up in the woods." He placed a
hand over his heart. "I knew it here. I felt his absence."

And Julie felt Forest's pain. It radiated out from
him, engulfing her in its depths. Despite the irratio-
nality of it all, she believed him. If something ever
happened to Bobby, she'd always thought she would
instantly know—that someplace in her heart, she
would feel it immediately.

"There's one thing you haven't mentioned, one
question you haven't answered," she said softly. He
waited, looking at her impassively. "Why?" she asked
softly. "Why would you have harmed Christopher?"

For a moment his shoulders remained slumped in
defeat and his eyes reflected a grief so deep it sent a
resounding ache through her. "I don't know," he finally said, and from the emptiness of his voice, she
realized that that fact more than anything haunted his
every moment. "I loved Christopher, but I hated Jeffrey. Jeffrey tormented me from the time I was small.
He hated me with all his heart, all his soul, and I responded in kind." He shrugged and straightened his
shoulders, the vulnerability vanquished along with his
expression of grief. "Jeffrey maintained that in a moment of madness, my hatred of him overcame my love
for Christopher. And I think that's exactly what hap-

pened.'' He didn't wait for her to reply, but instead turned and went up the stairs to his bedroom.

He moved across the darkened room to stand at the window, a lingering taste of bitterness in his mouth. Oh, God, it had been agony, reliving those moments.

He closed his eyes and went back…back to that day, that instant in time when his life had been ripped apart forever. After their morning of playing hide-and-seek, and a lunch of bologna sandwiches, Forest had sat down in the chair in front of the fire, and Christopher had stretched out on the floor. They had talked for a little while. Man talk, Christopher had always called it. He'd asked Forest why birds chirped, why girls giggled and if his mother was up in heaven looking down on him.

Christopher had finally drifted off to sleep. For a long time Forest had stared at the sleeping boy, his heart filled with a kind of love he'd never felt before. The loneliness he'd known as a child, with only a brother who hated him and a demanding, critical father, was eased by Christopher's love. It filled him so completely it frightened him at times. Then Forest must have fallen asleep, also.

Next thing he knew, he'd been alone in the woods, the sound of Christopher's screams echoing in his brain. What had happened? How had he gotten here? And where was Christopher? Heart pounding, terror tasting sour in his mouth, Forest had run for the house. He'd burst into the living room and stared at the place in front of the fire—the place where Christopher had been. Gone. He was gone.

Forest had run back outside, his head filled with Christopher's screams—screams of horror, screams of pain, screams that made Forest's blood run cold. Why had Christopher screamed? What had Forest done? Dear God, what had he done?

He'd called Jeffrey, who'd arrived moments later, and together they had searched the woods, looking for the little boy. Finally, the two had called the sheriff for help. While they'd waited for him to arrive, Jeffrey had exploded.

"What did you do to him?" he had screamed, wrapping his hands around Forest's neck. Forest had defended himself against the attack, wrestling out of his brother's grip and dodging wild blows.

"I don't know what happened," he had exclaimed. "I—I was asleep and he—he just disappeared." The words sounded weak even to his own ears.

"Liar," Jeffrey cried, the chords of his neck bulging. "You killed him, didn't you? You brought him out in the woods and killed him, then hid his little body."

"No!" Forest backed away from Jeffrey, horrified, yet filled with a weighty dread. "No! I love Christopher." Confusion swirled in his head. The screams . . . Christopher's screams.

"You bastard," Jeffrey spat. "You don't love him as much as you hate me. You've always hated me. I'm the real Kingsdon, I married MaryAnn and Christopher belongs to me. You couldn't stand it that he was mine. He was the only thing that mattered to me, and you killed him."

Forest's mouth had worked to form a denial, but no words had come. What Jeffrey'd said was true. There had been times when his hatred of his brother had been all-consuming. And why had he found himself standing in the forest, with Christopher's cries still echoing in his head?

He now opened his eyes. Outside, the storm had moved away, the lightning appearing halfhearted and tired. Each distant flash displayed the thick brush, the tangled undergrowth of the woods.

For the past ten years, every morning when he awakened and each night before he went to bed, Forest stood here at the window, staring into the woods. He had a feeling that if he stared long enough, concentrated hard enough, he would finally be able to remember exactly what had happened on that autumn afternoon so long ago.

He'd lied to Julie. He hadn't been asleep when Christopher disappeared. He'd experienced a blackout. That had been the first time it had happened. He didn't know how long it had lasted, or what he'd done while in the bizarre state of fugue. The only thing he knew for sure was that when he'd come to, he'd been standing in the woods, and somewhere in the dark recesses of his mind, Christopher's screams echoed. As Forest replayed those horrifying moments, he'd feared Jeffrey might be right.

The week following Christopher's disappearance had passed in a haze. Groups of townspeople had searched the woods, and Forest had talked to Orville Wolvertine, confessing what he feared, what Jeffrey had accused him of. "Hell, Forest, don't talk nonsense," the sheriff had protested. "Everyone in town knows how much you love that little tyke. The boy just wandered off, got lost. Don't worry, we'll find him."

But they hadn't, and after a month, everyone came to the conclusion that Christopher was probably dead. Jeffrey had left town a broken man, and Forest lived with a haunting guilt that ate at him day and night. As much as he wanted to deny it, he feared Jeffrey was right. In some sort of hate-induced fugue, he'd killed Christopher.

He turned away from the window, logically knowing that no matter how long he stood here and stared, Christopher wasn't going to magically walk out of the woods and make everything right. There was no way to go back and fix the past. Christopher's death had destroyed what little connection had existed between Forest and his brother. It had caused Forest to doubt his own sanity, to close himself off from everyone, to spend the last ten years hating himself more than anyone else could ever possibly hate a man.

He knew with certainty that Christopher's body remained in the woods. Someplace out there amid the tangled underbrush was the little boy he had loved, and Forest would never rest until he finally found him. He walked the woods each day, searching, looking, needing to find Christopher and give the child a proper burial. It was the least he could do. He'd spent the last ten years trying to figure out how to atone for a mortal sin he didn't remember committing but knew he had.

He stripped off his clothes and got into bed. He threw an arm across his eyes, shielding his gaze from the distant lightning. Sleep, he knew would be elusive, just as he knew that if he did manage to fall asleep, his dreams would be haunted ones.

It still bothered him that Julie had been able to hear the ghostly cries that for so long he had thought only he could hear. He'd always believed the cries were his own personal torment, the internal echo of his guilt. But if Julie could hear them, then the ghost was real, not just a figment of his tormented imagination.

He was afraid... not of the ghost, but of the blackouts, which he feared might cause another tragedy. He was afraid of what he might do to Julie, to Bobby. He was afraid that there was a murderer inside him, and that when he blacked out, that evil entity exploded in a killing rage. With Jeffrey's family once again in the house, Forest was deathly afraid.

Julie sat at the kitchen table, staring thoughtfully into a cup of coffee. Dawn was just breaking outside, but despite the early hour, Lottie had told her that Forest had already left for the mill.

"On Sunday?" Julie had asked in surprise.

"He goes in half days on Sundays, says it's the only time he can catch up on all the paperwork," Lottie had explained. The old woman had poured Julie a cup of coffee, then disappeared into the laundry room.

Julie stifled a yawn, then took a sip of her coffee. She hadn't slept well after her conversation with Forest. When she finally had fallen asleep, her dreams had been filled with the spectral vision of a little boy, thick woods and Forest.

The images of Forest had been as tangled as the woods that had surrounded her in the nightmarish landscape. One moment he had beckoned to her, his expression one of exquisite tenderness and eternal love. The next his face had been twisted with a murderous black rage, an overwhelming insanity, and his footsteps had crashed through the undergrowth as he'd chased her. In her dream, she was no longer Julie, but had somehow been transformed into Christopher, and she didn't know if she was running for her life, or merely playing a game of hide-and-seek.

She knew the dreams had been her unconscious attempt to work through the inconsistencies and lingering questions surrounding Christopher's disappearance and Forest's part in that tragedy.

She'd awakened no closer to having any answers. Her restless night had made her tired and cranky, and certain that Forest hadn't told her everything. She couldn't seem to get past the idea that somehow he believed that, while asleep, he had harmed Christopher.

People didn't kill while sleeping. Did they? She'd heard crazy stories of people on diets who wandered in the night, eating Twinkies and Moon Pies while deep in the throes of slumber. But she'd never heard of anyone killing somebody.

What had happened that day? What had happened to little Christopher? And what had happened to Forest that had made him so certain he'd killed the child? What was he hiding from her? What was he not telling her?

Julie got up from the table and poured herself another cup of coffee, the questions nagging insistently. Lottie bustled in with a laundry basket full of freshly dried clothes. The lemony scent of fabric softener filled the kitchen. The housekeeper placed the basket on one end of the table, then sat down and began folding the garments.

Julie sat down across from her and reached for one of the articles of clothing. "Now, now, missy. This is my job," Lottie protested.

"Please, let me help," Julie replied. "I'm not accustomed to spending my days doing nothing." She carefully folded one of Bobby's T-shirts. "Besides," she continued, "I'd like to talk to you."

"About what?" Lottie asked in surprise.

"About Christopher."

An expression of sadness pulled at Lottie's features. "Ah, the day he disappeared is the day the very life went out of this house." She took another T-shirt from the basket and meticulously folded it. "It destroyed what little relationship was left between Forest and Jeffrey."

"I've heard the two brothers weren't very close," Julie observed.

Lottie snorted. "That's the understatement of the century." She leaned back in her chair, laundry apparently forgotten for the moment. "Jeffrey was six years old when Richard brought Forest home. He didn't prepare Jeffrey in any way, just sprang a new baby brother on him. Jeffrey was used to being the king of the castle, so to speak, and he didn't cotton to sharing anything with Forest." Lottie paused a moment, her faded blue eyes distant with memories. "That Jeffrey, he was spoiled rotten, and he had a mean streak in him that often got him into trouble. There were times I feared he'd kill Forest before the youngster got big enough to defend himself. Still, I blame Richard for the way the boys got along."

"Their father? Why?" Julie asked, her hands reaching for another piece of clothing to fold.

"Richard liked competition, and he encouraged it between Forest and Jeffrey. As they got older, he often played them one against the other." Lottie sighed and ran a hand through her gray hair. "I think if left alone, those boys would have been fine together. For a long time Forest idolized Jeffrey, and if their father hadn't interfered, those two would have been as close as any two real brothers could be." Lottie raised her chin, a flash of fire in her eyes. "I told Richard once, told him he was ruining the both of them, the way he pitted them against each other, but he just laughed and said competition was healthy, good. He insisted it would make them both fighters and winners."

"How sad," Julie said, her heart expanding for the little boys who'd been conditioned to compete with each other, to hate each other. It scared her sometimes, what damage parents could do to their children in the name of love.

"I don't think Forest ever really forgave Jeffrey for marrying MaryAnn. She'd been Forest's sweetheart for over a year when Jeffrey managed to woo her away and marry her, lickety-split. Of course, in Jeffrey's defense, I think he loved MaryAnn, but I think he loved her more because Forest did, too. When she died, I thought Forest and Jeffrey would finally be able to put their differences behind them for the sake of that little boy. And for a while, they did."

"But it didn't last."

Lottie shook her head. "No, it didn't last. As Christopher got older, he adored Forest, and Jeffrey resented their closeness. Forest had a playfulness, a gentleness that Jeffrey didn't have, and it drew Christopher to his uncle like a bug to a light." She sighed, a heavy, sad exhalation of breath. "Then Richard died and things between Forest and Jeffrey got worse. They were fighting about the mill, fighting over Christopher. Usually I baby-sat the lad while Jeffrey was at work, but that particular week my sister was sick with a fearsome case of the flu, and I spent my time nursing her. Forest had been home since the accident that killed Richard. He'd taken a bad blow to the head and suffered a little dizziness. He wasn't well enough to be back at work, but he insisted he could watch Christopher while I was away."

"What do you think happened?" Julie asked, the laundry forgotten as she leaned forward. While she waited for Lottie to answer, she was aware of the ticking of the clock on the oven, the slight hum of the refrigerator.

Lottie frowned, and when she reached for another piece of the laundry, her hand trembled slightly. "I don't know, and I don't care to know. Jeffrey was crazy that day, saying all kinds of horrid things, and Forest was half-crazed as well." She sighed and pressed two fingers against her forehead, as if to ease a headache. "I like to think Christopher just wandered off. Christopher had a fascination with the woods. He'd gotten his butt whipped more than once for going off by himself.''

Julie frowned. "But Forest seems to think he did something to hurt Christopher in some way."

Lottie shrugged her shoulders and busied herself folding the last of the clothes, but Julie saw that the old woman's eyes were haunted with a tinge of fear. "That's between the man and his maker. It's true enough that there was bad blood between the brothers, but nobody really knows what happened that day."

Again Julie felt her head spinning. The discussion of the relationship between Forest and Jeffrey had only added fuel to the fire. Jeffrey had stolen Forest's girlfriend. Had that betrayal been the final straw, setting alight a seething rage that had festered for years? In a moment of explosive madness, had Forest harmed the one thing he knew Jeffrey held dear?

Lottie stood up, the basket of clothes neatly folded. "I'll put Bobby's things on your bed so I won't wake him," she said.

"Lottie, do you think Forest harmed Christopher?" Julie asked.

The old woman's face blanched and for a moment she didn't speak. "I'll tell you what I think. I think there's evil in this house." Before Julie could respond, she turned and disappeared out the door.

Julie expelled a deep breath and got up to pour herself a third cup of coffee. At this rate she'd suffer caffeine overdose before the sun was completely up in the eastern sky. Sipping the brew, she remained at the window, staring out into the woods.

Evil in the house? Was there evil in the house or in the man? What about the ghost? She suddenly thought of the eerie sobbing she'd heard. In all the drama of Forest's confession the night before, she had forgotten to tell him that she'd heard the pitiful crying just before he'd come up from the basement.

Was it possible that what she'd heard was the ghost of Christopher? Julie had certainly never thought much about ghosts, though she supposed that, someplace in the back of her mind, she didn't completely discount the possibility of such a thing. She had a very open mind when it came to things paranormal. She knew there was much that science couldn't explain, might never be able to explain.

If there really was a ghost, and the ghost was indeed Christopher, then why was he here? Didn't ghosts usually haunt because they were troubled souls not at rest? Was Christopher haunting this house because of Forest's presence? Was he haunting the man who had murdered him so long ago?

She shivered and curled her fingers around the warmth of her cup. That's all I need, she thought ruefully, to discover that Bobby and I are caught between a crazed murderer and a vengeful ghost.

She smiled, the shiver receding as she realized she was letting her overactive imagination sweep her away. There was absolutely no proof that Forest had murdered Christopher, and there was no proof that what she'd heard the night before had been the ghost of the little boy. And there's no proof that Forest is innocent, a tiny voice reminded her, only confusing the issue more deeply.

Leaning back in the chair, she replayed last night's conversation with Forest in her head. Why did he believe with such vehemence that he'd harmed Christopher? She knew there was something he wasn't telling, some secret that would make sense of all the madness. But what?

Sighing in disgust, she got up and poured the remainder of her coffee into the sink. She rinsed the cup and set it in the dishwasher, then left the kitchen.

She paused just outside the doorway that led down to the basement. Forest's workroom. He spent most of his time at home down there. What did he do? *Anything I want.* She remembered his answer. She wrapped her fingers around the doorknob, the cool metal reassuring as it turned easily beneath her grip.

Before she could think, before she could dissuade herself with good old common sense and caution, she opened the door and peered down the stairs.

The stairway was dark, the steps themselves narrow and steep, disappearing into utter blackness. She turned on the light switch and illuminated the stairs, walking down the first couple before she could change her mind. She needed to know. She needed to see exactly what was down here.

As she crept cautiously downward, her heart beat a rapid tattoo, resounding eerily in her ears. It made it seem like the basement had a heartbeat, and the heartbeat was in her head.

She reached the bottom of the staircase and stared at the door in front of her. She hesitated, feeling odd about invading Forest's privacy. But she had to know if there was something down here that would attest to his guilt...something that might be indicative of a monster inside him. Was there some kind of clue to his crime in this room? Some piece of evidence that made him soul-certain that he'd hurt Christopher? She had to know for herself. But more, she had to know for her son. Bobby was Jeffrey's child also, and if Forest was some kind of a monster who had hated Jeffrey with such passion, might Bobby be in danger?

Her heart was still thudding as she opened the door and stepped into the dark. She fumbled on the wall until she found a switch. Turning it on, she realized she stood in a large room. A workbench ran along one wall, a pegboard above it. There were electric saws, and tools she didn't recognize both on the bench and hanging on the wall. The floor was covered with wood chips and shavings, and the entire room smelled clean and fresh like Forest.

"What did you expect? Heads in jars? A freezer full of body parts?" she muttered in relief. Whatever she'd expected, it hadn't been the normal woodworking shop where she now stood.

Against one wall was metal, floor-to-ceiling shelving, and on those shelves was an array of carved items. Julie walked closer, marveling over the exquisite detail of each piece.

She picked up a figurine of a fox, the detail of the rich wood breathtaking. It was crouched as if ready to spring on its prey, its ears at attention. It looked so real, she half expected the woodland animal to sniff her hand. She carefully set the piece back and picked up another one, this one a wolf. As she ran a finger over the delicate carving, admiration swept through her... admiration for the obvious talent, the overwhelming patience and pure genius that had created each line.

She set the wolf down, her attention captured by a figurine that was separate from the others. It was a little boy on a rocking horse. The same rocking horse that now sat in Bobby's bedroom.

The boy on the horse looked to be about five years old. His hair was shaggy, as if he were between haircuts, and his mouth was open in what was obviously a burst of laughter. A dimple indented his left cheek and thick lashes enhanced his lively eyes.

Carefully Julie took the figure off the shelf, feeling the love that had gone into the carving. It flowed in the lines, radiated from the detail. A man who created such miracles with his hands couldn't destroy a human life. It wasn't possible that Forest could have carved this piece and been responsible for Christopher's death.

As Julie's hands reverently stroked the little statue, she knew with a gut-deep certainty that Forest did not have the capacity to harm anyone.

"What in the hell are you doing down here?"

Julie gasped in shock and whirled around to face Forest, whose features were twisted in anger. The certainty she'd felt only a moment before fled beneath the rage that emanated from him.

CHAPTER SIX

"I—I'm sorry." Julie felt a flush of heat stain her cheeks. "I—I shouldn't have come down here, but I was curious."

Forest didn't say anything for a moment, then he sighed resignedly. "Yes, that definitely seems to be one of your more-irritating character traits," he replied tightly. A muscle worked in his jaw. He walked over to where she stood and took the figurine out of her hands. He carefully placed it back on the shelf, then looked at her once again.

Julie took a step backward, away from his commanding presence. "I didn't know I had more than one irritating character trait," she said, trying to ease the uncomfortable tension that vibrated in the air.

"You have several." He took another step and stopped so close to her that she could feel the heat emanating from his body, see the gray flecks softening the darkness of his eyes. His lower jaw was shaded slightly with a growth of whiskers that only intensified his overt masculinity. Her breath was suddenly trapped in her chest, held captive by the heat of his gaze.

"Like what?" she finally asked breathlessly, aware that the anger that had pulled his features taut only moments ago was gone. Suddenly she realized it wasn't anger at all that she saw stirring in the depths of his eyes. It was something else, something that frightened her more than his rage. It beckoned to an answering emotion in her.

"Your hair looks so soft, so touchable, and I find that fact most irritating." He reached out and wrapped a strand of it around his thumb.

She knew she should turn and run...run as fast as she could away from the flaming warmth of his body, the hypnotic gaze of his eyes. And yet she found herself not wanting to escape. From the moment she had accidently stumbled upon him naked in his bedroom, she had fought the flicker of sexual desire that sparked in the pit of her very being. Now that flicker burst into an inferno, sweeping over her. Her body tingled from head to toe and made it impossible for her to turn and run. Impossible for her to do anything but stand and wait for him to take what he wanted from her.

He released the tendril of hair and with a single fingertip traced the line of her jaw. "And damn you, your skin looks soft as silk, and I find that irritating as hell," he whispered. The pad of his finger was slightly rough, and she wondered what it would feel like caressing her breasts, running across a turgid nipple. She gasped softly as his fingers stroked across her lips. Back and forth they moved, the tip of one delving slightly into the wetness of her mouth.

It was madness, pure craziness. This man had only last night confessed to possibly being a murderer. But Julie didn't want to think about that. Not here. Not now.

She closed her eyes and heard his desire in the way his breath quickened as he touched her mouth, caressed the curve of her jaw. Then his mouth was on hers, his lips demanding as his arms enfolded her against the length of him.

It was not a gentle kiss. It was a kiss of hunger, of urgency. It tasted of tortured loneliness and voracious need. Julie didn't fight against it. Instead she gave in to the wildness of the moment, realizing this was what she had wanted from the moment she had first met him.

His mouth was hot, his tongue dueling with hers as his arms pressed her closer to the contours of his body. She was aware of his arousal hot and hard against her abdomen, but it only fed the intensity of her own response to him. The force of his loneliness wrapped around her, called on the isolation she had felt not only in the past year, but all her life. She felt a completeness, as if in mating their feelings of loneliness, they banished them.

With a guttural groan, he tore his lips from hers and pushed her away. For a moment neither of them spoke. The room was filled with the sounds of their ragged breathing.

"I... Why did you do that?" she finally asked. She reached up to touch her mouth, aware that her lips were slightly swollen and throbbing from his kiss. And worse... she wanted him to repeat it. She wanted him to kiss her again and again and again.

His gaze made it impossible to guess what he was thinking. Black, obscured by the power of his own will, his eyes told her nothing. "Let's just say I de-

cided to indulge my own brand of curiosity,'' he finally said. ''You wanted to see my room. I wanted to
taste you.'' His eyes blazed once again with a hungry
fire that caused her heart to jump erratically. ''I want
you, Julie. I wanted you from the moment I opened
my door and saw you standing on my porch.''

She gasped as he pulled her to him again. She could
feel him, hot and rigid as he cupped her buttocks and
drew her intimately against him. A bitter smile played
over his sensual lips and he moved her body back and
forth against his, the friction creating an urgent heat
inside her. ''How would you feel about making love to
a murderer? There are some women who would find
the very idea titillating. Are you one of those, Julie?''
He released her once again and stepped away, his features taut with anger.

Beneath the brutality of his words, she heard the
forlorn tones of confusion, the emptiness of the
abandoned. ''What is this, Forest? Just another tech-
nique to try to make me run away? Leave here?'' She
ached with a need she couldn't define, the emptiness
back inside her, too. ''You can't make me leave, Forest. You can't make me leave with your anger, and you
can't make me leave with your sexual advances.''

''Get out of here, Julie. Leave me alone.'' He turned
away, as if he couldn't stand the sight of her.

''Forest?'' She placed a hand on his broad back,
realizing his anger wasn't directed at her. Self-loathing
rolled off him in waves, washing over her and making
her heart ache for him. ''Forest, I can't believe that
you did anything to hurt Christopher. You couldn't.

A man who creates such magic with his hands doesn't kill.''

He whirled around, his face twisted with the self-hatred she'd felt only moments before. "Magic? I'll show you magic.'' He grabbed her hand in a painful grip and pulled her across the room. He yanked open a cabinet door and pushed her closer.

Inside were more figurines. These weren't like the ones on the open shelves. These demanded the dark recesses of a closed cabinet. They were nightmarish figures carved by the dark side of the artist. Despite her abhorrence, Julie studied the pieces, repelled yet drawn to the beautiful horror of each one. Trees twisted and gnarled, with faces of demons on the trunks; a wolf with teeth bared, feral and danger-ous—each and every piece reflected nature at its most perverse, an ominous slant to the world.

He turned her around to face him, his eyes flaming with a soulless intensity that frightened her. He pulled her close to him, so close she could feel the heat of his breath on her face. "This isn't magic, Julie. It's mad-ness. Sheer madness.'' He laughed, and the madness rang in his voice, radiated from his eyes.

With a small cry she pulled out of his arms and ran up the stairs. His laughter followed her—the laughter of the damned.

Julie's perfume lingered in the air long after she had run out of the room. The light floral scent wrapped itself around him, penetrating his senses, piercing his soul.

Forest sank down on the stool in front of the work-bench, his head dizzy, his body trembling from the aftermath of the kiss. He shouldn't have kissed her. Dear God, he shouldn't have tasted the honeyed heat of her lips.

He'd forgotten. He'd forgotten the sweetness of holding a woman. He'd forgotten the feel of a wom-an's softness against his body, the hot mystery of a woman's mouth beneath his. Not any woman...Julie.

Her name exploded inside him, and he lowered his head into the cradle of his arms on the bench. The anticipation of that kiss had been building inside him since the moment she'd appeared on his doorstep. That night she'd looked so tired, so beaten, yet she'd had a hint of irrepressible pride sparking in her cara-mel-colored eyes. He'd felt an immediate ignition of attraction, an instantaneous burst of desire that had grown rather than diminished over the course of the week.

For the past ten years he'd been isolated from ev-eryone. Initially, it had been his tremendous grief that had kept people at bay, then it had been the misery of his guilt, the rumors and whispers that had kept him distant, separated from everyone in town. It hadn't taken long for loneliness and detachment from others to become a habit, a way of life.

But in a heartbeat Julie had changed all that. She'd made him remember the human need for love, the tactile pleasure of skin touching skin, mouths seeking heat, bodies moving in unison to the ancient rhythm of passion. She'd made him remember all the things he could never again have, all the things he no longer deserved. He remembered . . . and he wept.

"The only thing I really need you for is to answer the phones," Lorna explained to Julie on Monday morning. "I'm out of the office a lot and people are always calling in with items they think will make good stories. Just take their name and number and get an idea of what they're calling about."

Julie nodded and sat down at the desk in the small front room of the newspaper office. Lorna had already explained to her that the *Kingsdon Gazette* was a weekly, with a strictly local slant. She'd given Julie the official tour of the premises, which consisted of a large storage room with file cabinets from floor to ceiling. A portion of the room, partitioned off with more cabinets, was Lorna's office. The actual press resided in the basement.

"Oh, you should be getting a call sometime this morning from Edith Windslow. Just pretend like you're taking her name and number." Lorna grinned. "She calls every Monday to relate her experiences over the weekend in a UFO." Lorna leaned a hip against the desk. "According to Edith, the aliens pick her up every Friday night, spend the weekend conducting all kinds of examinations on her, then deposit her back in her bed Sunday night."

"Do you believe her?"

Lorna laughed. "I believe Edith is a lonely ninety-year-old woman who needs some excitement in her life. But no, I don't believe she's spending her weekends in a spaceship." She looked at her watch and stood up. "I've got to get out of here. I have an appointment in ten minutes with a lady who says she has a pumpkin that's shaped like Abraham Lincoln's head." She grinned. "It's a rough job, but somebody's got to do it." She grabbed a camera off a shelf. "I should be back before noon." With a wiggle of her fingers, she left the office.

Julie sat at the desk and looked around. Outside the large expanse of glass that formed the front of the office, the autumn sunshine cast a golden glow on Main Street. Up and down the street she could see signs of businesses being readied for a new day. An old woman swept the sidewalk in front of the grocery store. Shades across the windows of the hardware store moved upward, as if at the orchestration of an invisible hand.

Kingsdon was a nice town. The kind of place where Julie might have considered putting down roots. She didn't miss living in the city. She had often tried to convince Jeffrey to move out of New York City to a smaller community upstate.

Bobby was thriving here. He'd done more emotional healing in the week they'd been here than he had in the entire nine months since his father's death. If things were different, she would stay here. She and Bobby would become part of Kingsdon and revel in belonging. But things weren't different, and she knew she would eventually have to leave. Forest's kiss had changed everything.

Heat rose up inside her as she remembered his mouth on hers, the hardness of his body pressed intimately against her own. The kiss had rocked her to the core, evoked a heat of passion inside her she'd never before experienced.

Her and Jeffrey's physical relationship had always been rather tame. Although Julie had come into their marriage expecting passion and desire and the kind of physical intimacy only lovers could attain, it didn't take her long to realize Jeffrey wasn't a particularly passionate man. It didn't take her long to bury the passionate side of her own nature and settle for something less.

But Forest's kiss had reawakened that hunger, dormant for so long. She instinctively knew that Forest would never be satisfied with a woman who settled for less. He would demand response, expect the same kind of breathless passion he gave.

She jumped as the telephone rang, grateful for the interruption of her disturbing thoughts.

"Kingsdon Gazette," she said into the receiver, pen and paper ready to take a message. She put the pen down and smiled as Edith Windslow introduced herself and proceeded to relate her latest adventure aboard a martian spaceship.

The morning passed quickly. Surprisingly, there were a number of phone calls from citizens who had something they wanted announced. Mrs. Johnson, principal at the elementary school, called about a school carnival coming up in two weeks. Burt Simpkins wanted to put an ad in the paper for his drycleaning establishment. Several people called and left their names, with instructions for Lorna to call them back.

Lorna returned to the office just before noon. "Grab your purse and let's go get some lunch," she said as she breezed in.

"Shouldn't one of us stay here through the lunch hour?" Julie asked.

Lorna shook her head. "I always close up for an hour at noon. Everyone knows that if they have something that can't wait, they can find me at the café." She put the camera away and looked at Julie expectantly. "Come on, as a first-day-on-the-job treat, I'll buy your lunch."

"You don't have to do that," Julie protested as she followed Lorna out of the office into the noonday sunshine.

"You're right, I don't." Lorna grinned. "I'll just do it this once, and only if you order the special."

Julie laughed. "It's a deal."

The café was packed. Most tables were filled with burly men in flannel shirts who smelled of wholesome sweat and fresh-cut wood. Julie wasn't surprised. This was the only restaurant in a town too small to boast more than one fast-food place, a pizza parlor that delivered.

Julie and Lorna found a table in the corner and both ordered the meat loaf special from Betty.

"So, how was your morning?" Lorna asked, propping her elbows on the table as her gaze darted around the room, making flirtatious contact with several of the men.

"Actually, it was busier than I expected. I took several messages for you."

"Hmm, Monday mornings are always the same. The phone lines burn up with people wanting to get their names in the paper." Lorna wiggled her fingers at one particularly attractive blond man. "Martin Baylor," she said beneath her breath. "I have a date with him this Friday night."

"He looks nice," Julie observed.

"You should see him in a pair of cotton sweatpants and without a shirt."

Julie laughed as Lorna rolled her eyes and fanned herself with her napkin. Then she sobered slightly and took a sip of her water. "How long has the paper been in existence?"

"Forever," Lorna answered, giving Julie her full attention as Martin Baylor and his buddies paid for their lunches and left. "I've run it for the last five years. I bought it from Old Man Canterfield. He'd been editor and owner for the past twenty-five years."

"Are there copies of back issues anywhere? On microfilm?"

Lorna laughed. "You won't find any microfilm in this town, but I do have most of the old issues filed in those cabinets in the back room. Why?"

"Just curious," Julie said. "Would you mind if I looked through them in my spare time?"

Lorna shrugged. "Help yourself. Anything particular you're looking for?"

Julie shook her head, reluctant to tell Lorna exactly why she wanted to look at the old papers. "No, I just thought it might be a good way to really get to know the town and its people."

"Sure, you're welcome to look through whatever you want," Lorna replied.

The waitress brought their food, and they'd just begun to eat when another group of men walked in from the mill. Julie felt her breath tighten in her chest as she saw Forest among them. He nodded at the two women, then joined the men at a table nearby.

"You know, I had a massive crush on Forest when we were in high school," Lorna confessed as she smothered her meat loaf with catsup. "He was one of the heartbreakers of the school. Sinfully handsome but coolly aloof."

"Did you ever date him?" Julie asked, carefully keeping her gaze averted from him. Even the sight of him disturbed her, reminding her of the way his mouth had tasted, the feel of him so bold, so intimate against her.

"Nah, Forest was always too much man for me." Lorna grinned. "I like mine a little more agreeable, more malleable."

Julie laughed. "I can't imagine anyone being too much man for you."

Lorna's gaze went back to Forest and she frowned thoughtfully. "I don't want a man with a lot of angst. Forest is just too intense for my taste. If anyone is going to have emotional baggage in my relationships, it's going to be me!"

Again Julie laughed. There was something very likable about Lorna's irreverence toward herself and her love life. Julie wished she could be more like her boss and not take herself quite so seriously, but she couldn't.

Raised in a series of foster homes, she'd found the most important thing in her life when she'd been growing up was her dream of having a husband and a family. Unfortunately, her marriage had not fulfilled many of her expectations. She now realized that Jeffrey, having lost a family once before, had probably been afraid of the degree of intimacy Julie had desperately needed out of the relationship. Their marriage had likely been doomed from the very start.

Julie looked back at Forest, once again replaying his kiss in her mind. It had held nothing back, had demanded that she relinquish all of herself, and for those few moments when his lips had claimed hers, she had.

She had a feeling that Forest would expect and demand total acquiescence of body, mind and soul, and there was a part of her that hungered for that. Another part was frightened by the thought of such total surrender.

"So are you and Bobby planning on staying permanently in Kingsdon?" Lorna asked, pouring another huge dollop of catsup over the remaining piece of her meat loaf.

"I'm not sure," Julie answered truthfully. "Right now I'm just kind of taking things one day at a time. To be perfectly honest, part of what brought us here was the fact that Jeffrey left us completely broke." She felt a flush of embarrassment sweep over her face. "I didn't realize how far in debt we were until bill collectors came and took nearly everything we owned."

"Oh, hon," Lorna said sympathetically. "Bad enough to find yourself a young widow, but a broke widow at that..."

"Things could be worse," Julie said. "At least we had a place to come to, and now I have a job, and before long Bobby and I will be firmly back on our feet."

"And I hope you'll stay here in Kingsdon for a very long time." Lorna toyed with her fork for a moment, then looked at Julie once again. "Although I have to admit, I'd feel better if you could find another place to live." She leaned over the table. "There have always been whispers about that house, and Forest."

"You mean because of Christopher?"

Lorna nodded. "Did you ask Forest about him?"

"Yes, although he was reluctant to talk about it," Julie admitted.

Lorna shook her head. "It was such a tragedy. It really split the town apart. The men at the mill were already divided into two camps, those who followed Jeffrey and those who followed Forest." She twirled her fork and looked at Julie once again. "There were some who believe Forest did something horrible to Christopher, that he wanted to break Jeffrey completely."

"That's ridiculous," Julie exclaimed uneasily. She still didn't know what to believe, but she wasn't about to discuss the issue with the woman who owned the local paper. She wasn't going to be the one to feed the Kingsdon grapevine. Lorna seemed to get the hint and concentrated on her food.

They ate for a few more minutes in a companionable silence. Julie was acutely conscious of Forest's presence in the room. It was as if her eyes were magnets and he were a sheet of metal. No matter where she tried to look, her gaze was drawn back to him.

She knew he felt her, too. Each time her gaze was pulled to him, his eyes looked at her. It was like a childish game of peekaboo, with first one, then the other quickly looking away.

Julie was almost grateful when she and Lorna finished eating. As they got up to leave, Julie was aware of Forest's gaze once again. She could feel it lingering on her, hot and hungry, as she walked out of the cafe.

"Lorna, do you believe in ghosts?" she asked as they walked back to the newspaper office.

"Ghosts?" Lorna looked at her in surprise. "You mean like spirits who rattle chains and haunt cemeteries?" She shook her head. "Nah, not me. I don't believe in any kind of supernatural garbage. Why?"

"Oh, just curious, that's all."

Lorna looked at her skeptically. "Just curious, huh? You'd better lie to me better than that. I'm a newspaper woman, remember? I've got a nose for stories, and my nose is definitely twitching at the moment."

Julie laughed uncomfortably, somehow sorry she had brought the subject up. "It's probably nothing."

"Come on . . . give," Lorna demanded.

"Twice since being in Kingsdon Manor, I've heard a strange sound."

"What kind of a sound?" Lorna unlocked the office door and they went inside. Julie sat down behind her desk and Lorna pulled up a chair in front of her. "What kind of noise did you hear?" she repeated.

"Crying. The sound of a child crying." Julie smiled self-consciously. "I know it sounds crazy, but I think it might have been the ghost of Christopher Kingsdon."

Lorna stared at her wordlessly for a long moment, then threw back her head and laughed. "Oh, Julie, you don't really believe that, do you?"

Julie flushed hotly. "I know what I heard," she protested. "I heard a child crying. It wasn't Bobby and it sounded eerie, otherworldly... like a ghost."

"But I got the impression that Forest wasn't too thrilled when you showed up on his doorstep."

"That's true, but what does that have to do with anything?" Julie asked with a frown.

Lorna smiled patiently. "Have you considered the fact that those noises might have been made on purpose, so that you'd think you'd heard a ghost and would hightail it right out of that house?"

Julie opened her mouth to protest, then frowned again. Was that possible? When she'd written Forest to see if it would be okay for her and Bobby to come here, he'd never answered her. She knew how disagreeable he had been when she'd first shown up at the house. It had been he who had first planted the idea of a ghost in her head. Was it possible that he manufactured those eerie noises to frighten them away? Had she heard the ghost of Kingsdon Hill, or had she heard the madman of Kingsdon Hill?

CHAPTER SEVEN

Forest sat at his workbench, trying to focus on the carving he held in his hands instead of on the woman who seemed to invade his every thought. Julie. Her very name was a litany of torment that caused fire in his veins. She'd stirred a hunger in him, a hunger that had been denied for far too long.

He frowned and ran his hand over the piece of wood, then picked up a sheet of fine sandpaper and began working it back and forth across the surface.

He hesitated as he heard the whisper of a footstep on the stairs, smelled the scent of sun-warmed hair and bubble gum. He felt a prickling at the small of his back and knew somebody was watching him. He knew immediately it was the boy. Bobby.

He swiveled around on the stool and saw him peeking around the corner of the door. "What are you doing there?"

Bobby stepped into the room hesitantly, his gaze darting about with curiosity. He shrugged and kept his eyes averted from Forest's. "Mom told me you made stuff down here." He took a step closer to the shelves. "Wow, did you make this stuff?"

Forest fought his initial impulse to bellow at the boy to get out. Since the moment Julie had arrived at the house with Bobby, he'd kept himself distant from him, not wanting to care, not wanting another child to get into his heart.

Still, as he looked at Bobby, he realized he didn't want to send him away. The little-boy scent filled the room like a haunting memory from the past and he could feel the unbridled energy coming from the child. "Does your mother know you're down here?" he asked.

Bobby shook his head and frowned. "She told me to stay away from here." The frown disappeared as he looked again at the wood carvings on the shelves. "Did you make the big rocking horse that's in my room, too?"

Forest nodded. "A long time ago."

Bobby moved closer to where Forest sat. "Could you teach me how to carve stuff?"

Forest looked at him in surprise. Christopher had often liked to play down here while Forest worked, but he'd never expressed any interest in learning how to carve.

"I'd like to learn how to carve a fox like that." Bobby pointed to the wooden fox on the shelf.

"Before you can carve a fox, you should be able to draw one." Forest knew he was taking a chance, knew he shouldn't be anywhere near the boy, but at the moment his need was greater than his fear. He needed to go back to that time years ago, when he'd found the magic of childhood with a special little boy.

He pulled another chair up to the bench and motioned Bobby into it. He then withdrew some paper from a drawer and set it and a pencil before Bobby.

"You draw me a picture of a fox and we'll see what we have to work with."

"Okay," Bobby agreed enthusiastically. He immediately began sketching, pausing occasionally to scratch the end of his nose or erase an errant mark. "Did my dad know how to carve?" he asked.

At the thought of Jeffrey, Forest's stomach clenched as if a tight vise gripped it. No, your father only knew how to hurt, how to taunt, how to hate. And he taught me to do the same. "No, your father didn't carve," he answered.

"Who taught you how to do it?" Bobby asked, his attention still absorbed in the picture he was drawing.

"Nobody. I just taught myself."

"Cool." Bobby looked up and smiled at Forest, an open, wonderful smile.

Forest began working the sandpaper back and forth on the chunk of wood in his hand, his thoughts whirling. Were all kids so open, so automatically accepting? That was one of the things that had always amazed him about Christopher. Children were naturally nonjudgmental, naturally giving. What had happened to Jeffrey and him? How had their childhoods been so twisted, their characters so perverted? How had hate become such a constant thing between them?

He looked back at Bobby, noting how, when the boy concentrated, he caught his tongue between his teeth. Forest did that, too. It must be a Kingsdon trait. Ah...family. This child was part of Forest's family; his own blood ran through him. Forest's heart ached at the loss of another boy... and with the knowledge that he could never allow himself to be close to this child. He couldn't put another son of Jeffrey's in danger. He couldn't put his own heart at risk again.

"What do ya think?" Bobby held up his completed picture. Forest took it from him and looked at it critically, surprised that the boy displayed a natural talent.

"Not bad. Here, let me show you something." Forest grabbed another pencil and erased the ears that Bobby had sketched. "You've drawn him ready to pounce, but the ears are wrong. They need to be more alert...like this." Forest quickly began redoing them. He'd completed one when he felt it—the sensation of cold air on the back of his neck. His nose became filled with the scent of the woods, the smell of thick vegetation and slightly rancid mulch.

Alarm swam through him. He knew what was about to happen. It was always the same. He shoved away from the bench, his stool crashing to the floor behind him. "Get out of here, Bobby."

He was vaguely aware of the little boy staring at him in frozen fear. He was also conscious of a seeping darkness at the fringes of his vision, a darkness attempting to swallow his consciousness. "Run, Bobby, run!" he gasped desperately, and breathed a ragged sob of relief when the boy's momentary paralysis broke and he scampered up the stairs.

Forest sank down on the floor, head in hands, hoping the child had run fast enough, far enough. Then the blackness descended completely, and he knew no more.

* * *

"Whoa!" Julie exclaimed as Bobby ran into her in the kitchen. "Hey, what's your hurry?" She held him by the shoulders. His eyes were huge as he looked up at her. "Bobby? Is something wrong?"

"Uh, no, nothing's wrong." He squirmed in her firm grip. "I've just got to go to the bathroom."

She eyed him sharply, with the natural instinct of a mother.

"Mom, really. I've got to go." He wiggled out of her grasp and darted away from her, up the stairs.

Julie stared after him. She didn't know what was wrong, but she knew what Bobby's bathroom look was, and that hadn't been it. She suddenly realized that he had come from the direction of the basement stairs. Had he been downstairs in Forest's workroom? She'd told him time after time not to go down there, not to bother his uncle.

She decided to get to the bottom of things and went in search of Bobby. She caught him by the shoulders as he barreled out of the bathroom. "Were you downstairs with Uncle Forest?"

Bobby's face grew pale with guilt. He hesitated, then nodded his head. "I just wanted to see what he did down there all the time."

"I told you not to go down there, young man."

"Don't worry, I won't again," Bobby assured her in a way that was distinctly unreassuring.

"Why? What happened?"

Bobby's eyes widened and his bottom lip jutted out slightly. "It was okay at first. He was kinda nice and told me to draw him a picture. Then all of a sudden he changed, and he yelled and told me to run away. His face was all mean and I ran. I won't go down there anymore, Mom. I promise.''

Julie didn't know whether to spank him or hug him. She opted for a hug and held him close for a moment. ''Didn't you tell me you had some math homework tonight?''

''Aw, Mom,'' Bobby protested.

She pointed in the direction of his room. ''Go on. Do your homework, then clean up that room.'' She watched until he disappeared through the doorway of her bedroom, then she turned and went back downstairs to the kitchen. She walked over the window, disturbed by what Bobby had told her.

Forest had been nice, then had suddenly changed. His face had turned mean looking. What Bobby had said replayed in her mind. Was it merely a case of a man being impatient with a little boy's snooping? Or was it something darker, more sinister? She shivered and stepped away from the window, suddenly terribly afraid.

''See you Monday,'' Julie said to Lorna as she left the newspaper office on Friday afternoon. She walked outside into the waning autumn sunshine, moving in the direction of her car.

It had been a good week but a tiring one. She'd forgotten how hectic life could be when working at a full-time job and dealing with a seven-year-old. Still, it was a good kind of tired. For the first time in a long while, she felt like she was actively working at her life, not just letting it roll her along like a tumbling rock.

She climbed into her car and cranked down the window, for a moment just sitting and relaxing as she contemplated the last five days. Not only was she answering the phones, but Lorna now had her writing some of the news stories and laying out ads. She and Lorna were quickly developing a nice friendship despite their differences in philosophy and experience. They often spent their lunch hours indulging in lively discussions and arguments about men, marriage and politics.

Julie was enjoying every aspect of her new job, and at noon that day had opened a bank account and deposited most of her first paycheck. She now sighed with satisfaction and started the engine of the car.

The thought of the evening ahead filled her with anticipation. Bobby was spending the night with one of his new friends, and Julie was looking forward to a long soak in a bubble bath and an early bedtime to recuperate from the long week.

As she drove through town, her thoughts turned, as they often did, to Forest. She'd scarcely seen him all week, but that didn't matter. Out of sight was definitely not out of mind where he was concerned. Since their kiss, he had occupied far too much of her thoughts during the day, and at night he possessed her dreams. They were erotic dreams that reached into the core of her being and lingered for several long, exquisite moments after she awakened.

True to his word, Bobby hadn't ventured down to the basement workshop again, and Julie had decided that Forest had merely exhibited the irascibility of a man who didn't want to be bothered.

Despite the fact that everything seemed to be going well, Julie felt like she was functioning with her breath held. She went to bed with an air of expectation and awoke with the same sense of weighty anxiety. She wasn't sure what she expected to happen, but knew that the house itself seemed to radiate a tension that filled her with a curious sense of dread. She felt as if she were waiting for a shoe to drop and had already been warned that it was going to land directly on her head.

At least there had been no more ghost sounds during the last week. She still didn't have any idea if what she'd heard had really been the ghost of Christopher Kingsdon, or an orchestrated attempt to scare her off. It didn't matter either way. For the moment she wasn't going anywhere. Until she had enough money to finance a new start someplace else, she and Bobby were stuck right where they were.

She pulled her car up in front of the house, struck as always by the darkness that shrouded the dwelling. Despite the golden glow of twilight, which painted the tops of the trees in lush tones, the saffron light did nothing to alleviate the shadows that possessed the place. It was as if the house itself repelled the light, preferring the nighttime.

It seemed a reflection of Forest. The house, like the man, appeared lifeless, without hope, devoid of a soul. There was an emptiness of spirit both in the man and in the house where he lived. "Silly woman," she muttered to herself as she parked the car and got out. She definitely needed a restful night...a night without dreams.

When she went inside, she found Lottie in the kitchen preparing the evening meal. "It's going to be an hour or so before we eat," the older woman said. "The roast is taking longer than I expected it to," she explained.

"That's all right with me," Julie replied. "We had a late lunch today, and I'll use the hour to unwind a little bit." She went upstairs, anxious to get out of her panty hose and skirt and into a comfortable pair of jeans.

Once changed, she decided to sit on the back patio for a while and enjoy the last gasp of fall. The trees that last week had been bedecked in splendid autumn dress had begun their yearly striptease, shedding colorful leaves and baring stark limbs.

The patio consisted of a small area of brick and cracked concrete that held rusted, wrought-iron furniture. She assumed it hadn't been used in years. Julie moved one of the chairs so that it faced the woods, which loomed dark and primal at the edge of the overgrown lawn.

She spotted the break in the undergrowth that she knew was the beginning of the path Forest took on his way to work each morning. Funny, she'd been here two weeks and had yet to explore any of the surrounding, wooded territory. And soon winter would grip the area, making a walk in the woods much less desirable.

She got up from her chair, suddenly wanting to follow the path that Forest walked every day. Why did he walk to work? Why didn't he drive down the hill to the mill? What lure did the woods hold for him?

She went back to the kitchen door and called to Lottie. "I'm going to take a walk. I'll be back in a little while."

"If you're walking in the timber, don't you go off that path. There're deep ravines and fallen trees all over the place."

"Don't worry," Julie assured her. "I have no intention of going off the beaten path."

Julie quickly discovered that the beaten path was difficult enough. Although it started out fairly wide and lit with the pale golden hues of the evening sun, it soon narrowed. The trees crowded together, their limbs forming barriers overhead that blocked out the sun and muted all sound. Here no wind rustled the leaves, no wild animals scurried. There was nothing but forest, black and impenetrable.

The air was cooler, and even though Julie knew that colors had no odor, it smelled *green*...like tangled vines and slippery moss and thick weeds. As she walked, she passed some of the ravines Lottie had warned her about—steep ditches that appeared to plunge into dark nothingness. She shivered and moved to sit on a fallen tree trunk along the path.

Christopher. She still found it difficult to realize Jeffrey had once had another wife, another son—a family and a life he'd lost through tragic events. It was no wonder she'd always sensed a certain amount of emotional detachment from him. She realized now that he'd probably been afraid to care too deeply, afraid to love too much, afraid that he would lose again. Christopher's death had taken its toll on her as well as Forest and Jeffrey. Her failed marriage had been a victim of the past and its tragic circumstances.

She frowned, aware of the sound of footsteps drifting to her from someplace up ahead. Unsure exactly what it was she heard, she stood up and moved forward cautiously, trying to be as quiet as possible. She stopped again and listened intently. Yes, it was definitely the sound of footsteps crunching the flooring of dead leaves and grass. It seemed to be coming from an area just to the left of the path where she stood.

She parted the thick brush, startled to see Forest pacing back and forth in a small clearing. She started to call his name and move forward to greet him, then hesitated. Something was wrong. She stepped back amid the brush, frowning as she stared. Something was wrong with Forest. His gait was slow, almost dreamlike as he paced back and forth.

But it was his face that captured her attention. It was completely unlined, unnaturally devoid of expression . . . empty of any emotion. As he turned back to face her once again, he looked right at her, yet there was no indication that he saw her. His face remained passive, untroubled, and in that instant she saw the beauty that his features could possess without the torment, the haunted look that was always there.

Still, it disturbed her, the utter passivity, the strange jerkiness, the repetitive motions. It wasn't normal. It was the same thing she'd seen briefly that day in the kitchen. As she watched, he suddenly stopped pacing. He looked around the clearing, his gaze wild, the torment back in his eyes, twisting his features.

Instinctively Julie melted deeper into the brush, not wanting him to see her, knowing he wouldn't want to find her watching him. He looked down at his wristwatch, then hissed a curse, the sound exploding the silence and causing Julie to stumble backward. She turned and ran silently back up the path.

It didn't take her long to get to the house, where she threw herself into the wrought-iron chair on the patio and tried to catch her breath. What had she just witnessed? What had he been doing? Why had he looked like he was on drugs or in a strange trance?

Thoughts whirled in her head as she watched the entrance to the path, expecting him to emerge at any moment. He'd looked so peculiar, like a malfunctioning robot. *The porch light is on, but nobody is home.* The old adage came to mind and she realized it fit perfectly. For a moment, as he'd paced back and forth, he'd been nothing more than a vacant shell, absolutely empty inside.

She remembered a night long ago when she and Jeffrey had gone to a club and watched the stage show of a hypnotist performing on volunteers from the audience. She'd watched with interest as he'd worked his magic on the six people who had come forward. When they were hypnotized, they had all worn the same expression Forest had, as if all the emotions had been emptied out of them.

But there had been no hypnotist in the woods. So what had Forest been doing? What had caused the strange blankness that had momentarily gripped him?

She jumped as he emerged from the path, a dark scowl on his face. The scowl seemed to intensify as his gaze fell on her. "What are you doing out here?" he asked.

"It was such a beautiful evening I decided to take advantage of it." She was glad her voice sounded normal and didn't reflect the turmoil of her inner thoughts.

To her surprise, he grabbed a chair and pulled it up near hers, then sat down. For a moment he didn't speak, and his gaze lingered on the woods. The last golden light spilled down on the tops of the trees, and the sky had filled with deeper oranges and purples.

She watched him, trying to summon the nerve to confess that she'd seen him in the woods, that she'd noticed something odd. But as always, his expression invited no entry into his personal thoughts. Besides, she reasoned, perhaps it had been nothing more than the fact that he'd been deep in thought. Maybe she'd only imagined the utterly empty expression on his face.

"It won't be long before the snow falls," he said.

"I'll bet it's beautiful when all the trees are covered with snow." Julie looked back at the woods, trying to imagine it frosted with snow and gleaming with ice crystals.

He turned and looked at her. "Beautiful?" He sighed and gazed back at the woods. "I suppose some would find it beautiful." His features pulled tight again. "For me it's never beautiful. It's harsh and lonely and—" He broke off and stood up. "I'm sure Lottie has dinner ready."

Julie nodded and followed him inside. They ate in silence. Normally Bobby filled in the blanks in the mealtime conversation, telling Julie about his day at school and his friends. Forest rarely added anything to the conversation, although he never seemed to mind Bobby's childish prattle.

They'd almost finished eating when, to Julie's surprise, Forest asked about Bobby. "Where's the boy?"

Julie frowned irritably. "Why do you have so much trouble with his name? He isn't just some boy, he's your nephew, and he's spending the night with a school friend." She sliced into her roast beef more viciously than necessary, her anger rising too quickly to control. "I find exceedingly irritating the way you keep your distance from him by refusing to even speak his name. It's one of the many things I find irritating about you," she added.

His dark eyebrows rose and a mocking smile curved his sensual lips. "You mean I have more than one irritating characteristic?"

She blushed hotly, suddenly remembering that a very similar conversation had preceded the explosive kiss they'd shared. He seemed to remember the same thing, for his arrogant smile faded and he frowned down at his plate. "So who is his school friend?"

"Roger Courtland. Lottie told me the Courtlands are a very nice family, and I spoke with Mrs. Courtland this morning to make sure she was aware of the boys' plans."

He nodded. "The Courtlands are a nice family. Bill is one of my foremen at the mill, and his wife works part-time at the library."

"I'd like to visit the mill sometime. I'd like Bobby to see it," Julie said.

"Why?" He gazed at her dispassionately.

Julie shrugged. "I don't know. I've never seen a mill before, and it's part of the Kingsdon heritage."

"Don't you have any heritage of your own?" he asked brusquely.

"As a matter of fact, I don't." Julie's stomach knotted as childhood memories swept through her. Memories of loneliness, and the feeling of not belonging to anything or anyone. She took a sip of her water, then continued, "I have no idea who my father was, and my mother died when I was two years old. I don't remember her at all. My heritage is a series of foster homes, some good, some bad."

"You had no other family?" Forest asked.

Julie shook her head. She wanted to tell him that that was probably why she'd jumped almost immediately into marriage with Jeffrey. She'd had an enormous need to create a family for herself, and it was only now that she understood the distance Jeffrey had maintained would have eventually destroyed their marriage, had he lived. She'd needed more from him than he could give.

She picked up her water glass and took another sip, then looked at Forest, needing him to understand why he and his background was so important to her, and to Bobby. "I know the emptiness I've always felt. Like a drifting boat with no anchor, no port. I don't want Bobby to feel that. I want him to know his roots, understand his heritage."

Forest shoved his empty plate away, the darkness back in the depths of his eyes. "His grandfather was a philanderer, his father was a ruined man and his uncle is a madman.'' He stood up. ''Some heritage the kid is getting.'' He stalked out of the room, leaving Julie alone in the sudden, overwhelming silence of the house.

CHAPTER EIGHT

Although it was not quite eight o'clock when Julie finished her bath, she pulled on her nightgown and crawled into bed. The hot bubble bath had relaxed her and she knew sleep was only a blink away. She yawned and turned out the bedside lamp, then snuggled into the sheets and closed her eyes.

A knock sounded on the door. "Just a minute," she called out. She stumbled from the bed and turned on the lamp, then answered the door. Forest was there.

"I'm sorry, I didn't realize you were ready for bed." His gaze flickered darkly as it played over the length of her. Bold and hot, it lingered here, caressed there. Her nightgown suddenly felt like molten silk, as if the heat of his eyes caused it to smolder and adhere to every curve of her body.

"What do you want?" She licked her lips, her mouth suddenly dry as her body vibrated with expectation, anticipation... of what, she didn't know.

"This is Bobby's." He held out a sheet of paper, a drawing of some sort. As she took it from him, their fingers touched, and Julie felt a jolt of electrical current sizzle through her.

She looked down at the picture blankly. "What is it?" she asked, trying to forget the fact that they were all alone in the big house, that her flesh was on fire with a hunger she knew only he could satisfy.

"Bobby drew it, and he had the ears all wrong. I fixed them." His voice sounded strange, husky with suppressed emotion. She knew the memory of their kiss burned in him as hotly as it did in her. That kiss had stoked a fire so intense she knew there was no way to put it out. The only solution was to let it flame freely until eventually it burned itself out entirely. "I ran across it in my workroom just a little while ago and thought Bobby might want it back."

She nodded. She knew that a single touch from him would cause her to spiral out of control. She wanted to lose herself in the shadows of his eyes, surrender to the frenzied need inside her.

He backed away, as if he saw the fire inside her and was unwilling to commit himself to the flames. "Good night," he said tersely, then disappeared down the long, dark hallway.

She released a shaky sigh and closed the door. Her heart ached with the intensity of desire that pounded through her. What was she going to do with this flood of wanting? How on earth was she supposed to survive this gnawing need? She'd never wanted a man like she wanted Forest.

It wasn't until she got back into bed that she realized Forest hadn't called Bobby "that boy," but instead had referred to him by name. Surely that was a good sign, a sign that he was starting to accept his nephew.

She turned out her lamp and rubbed her forehead tiredly. God, things were so confusing. She didn't know whether to be glad or afraid that Forest might get closer to Bobby. She didn't know whether she was putting herself and her son in jeopardy by being here or not. She only knew that at the moment there were too many questions and not enough answers to satisfy her.

The air around her suddenly seemed too warm. She kicked off the blankets and tried to keep her thoughts away from Forest. Damn the man for being so attractive, for possessing eyes that promised exquisite sins. Damn the man for giving her that soul-searing kiss.

She tossed and turned until nearly midnight, by which time she was so frustrated she wanted to scream. She'd been exhausted when she'd gotten into bed, but Forest's brief visit had chased all sleep away.

She sighed again and sat up, realizing it was ridiculous to lie in the dark and wait for sleep to claim her. Turning on the lamp, she reached for the paperback book she'd bought during her lunch hour that day. Surely if she read for a little while, she'd finally be able to shove away all thoughts of Forest and fall asleep.

Plumping her pillow up behind her back, she opened the murder mystery and began to read. She'd read only a few pages when the lamp next to the bed flickered off, then back on. She leaned over and checked the bulb, making certain it was screwed in tightly. At the same moment she became aware of a chill that gripped the room. It was more than a chill. The room was icy cold, and the premonition of dread that had filled her for the last week returned, this time exploding inside her as she sat unmoving on the bed.

Her chest rose and fell with each labored breath. She felt her heartbeat increase in rhythm, and the palms of her hands were suddenly sweaty.

A frigid finger of air stirred along her bare arms, raised the hairs on the nape of her neck and rippled across her face. As it swept over her she filled with immeasurable loneliness. Sadness overwhelmed her, swallowed her.

She was consumed with an ache of such loss. Alone...she was so alone. She gasped as the lamp flickered off and on once again, and she realized tears were spilling down her cheeks, tears she didn't understand but couldn't stop. She only knew that she was lost, abandoned and frightened by the intense, hollow desolation that swept through her in wave after agonizing wave.

As quickly as it began, it ended. The loneliness immediately dissipated, although her body still shook with uncontrollable tremors.

She pulled the blanket up closer around her, her fingers shaking as she placed the book she'd been reading on the table next to the bed. What had just happened? She rubbed her hands over her eyes, finding remnants of her tears still wet on her cheeks. Had she fallen asleep for a moment and merely dreamed it all?

"No," she whispered in answer to her own question. She hadn't been asleep. The flickering lamp had been real. The cold air that had drifted over her like the horrifying caress of the dead...it had all been real. In fact, the room was still unnaturally cold. So cold.

The lamp blinked off again, plunging the room into darkness, and she tensed, unsure what to expect, but knowing to expect something.

An enormous boom resounded. Julie screamed and jumped from the bed, terror riveting through her. The noise erupted once again, and a picture crashed to the floor as the walls shook from the roar. Without waiting another moment, afraid that the walls themselves were tumbling down, she ran out into the dark hallway, where she met Forest. "What is it?" she asked breathlessly. "What's going on?"

"I—I don't know." His voice sounded strained, tense. He grabbed one of her hands. "Come on, I've got a flashlight in my room." Together they moved down the dark hallway and into his bedroom, where moonlight spilled in through the windows, painting the masculine furniture in ghostly illumination.

He led her to the bedside table, where he released her hand, opened the drawer and withdrew a large flashlight. He clicked on the high-power beam and, absurdly, Julie felt better, safer. Surely a powerful flashlight and Forest could protect her from things that went bump in the night. "I'm going downstairs to look around," he said softly.

"I'll come with you," Julie exclaimed, not about to be left alone in the dark.

Together they crept down the stairs. Julie clung to Forest's arm as the flashlight pierced the blackness before them. They had gone halfway down the stairs when the booming began again. It reverberated through the house, seeming to come from nowhere and everywhere. It surrounded them, engulfed them.

Julie flew into Forest's arms, clutching him as the walls, the roof, the house around them exploded in sound. Cold air enveloped them. Their breaths were expelled in vaporous mists that swirled like frantic spirits in front of them. The stairway vibrated beneath their feet, as if threatening to blow apart and cast them to the ground below.

Julie hid her head against his chest. She squeezed her eyes closed, afraid of what she might see, horrified by the thunderous booms that ripped the air around them. They came in patterns of five. Five booms, then a moment of silence, then five more.

"What is it? What is it?" Julie screamed, wanting to press the palms of her hands against her ears to block out the noise, but afraid to release the death grip she had on Forest.

"I don't know," Forest said again, his voice strained and nearly inaudible amid the deafening pandemonium. Wave after wave of sound assaulted them, as frosty air embraced them.

Julie didn't know how long they stood there. Time lost all meaning. She kept her head tucked against Forest's chest, focusing only on the feel of his beating heart and the fresh, minty scent of soap and masculinity. Those were the only normal things in a world gone mad. Around them reality had stopped and horror reigned, and Forest was a warm, safe center.

The very air surrounding them was oppressive, filled with an unnatural pressure that made her want to scream again. Her sanity was slipping and she hugged Forest more tightly. She wanted to crawl inside him and hide there.

"It's over."

Julie didn't move, but whimpered into the hollow of his neck, her eyes still tightly closed.

"Julie." He gently moved her away from him. "It's over."

"Are you sure?"

"Can't you tell?" He stepped back.

Yes, whatever it was, it was over. The air around them was warm again. Normal. She could see the light of her bedside lamp spilling from the doorway into the hall. The pressure, the tension she'd felt surrounding them was gone. Yes, at least for the moment she knew he was right. It was over.

"Let's go downstairs and see what we can find." Forest clicked off the flashlight as he turned on the hall light. They cautiously descended the rest of the stairs, both expecting to find complete destruction in the rooms below.

Nothing. They searched each and every room, but found no aftermath, no evidence of anything amiss. Despite the thundering noise that had crashed through the house, they found nothing broken in any of the rooms.

"I don't understand," Julie said as she sank down onto the sofa. "We weren't hallucinating. Those noises were real. It sounded like the house was falling down...like a wrecking ball was slamming into the roof, the walls."

"I don't know what to think," Forest admitted. He sat in his chair before the fireplace and leaned forward with his head in his hands. A muscle in his jaw worked like a misplaced heartbeat, letting Julie know he was more disturbed than he acted.

"Has anything like this happened before?"

He shook his head. "Never."

Julie frowned, searching for rational explanations for the strange phenomena they had just experienced. "There isn't some sort of military base nearby, is there? Or an airport? Maybe they were sonic booms." She flushed as he raised his head and eyed her wryly. "Is there some sort of a fault line under the house? Or an underground river?" Her flush deepened. "Well, I'm trying to think of rational explanations," she said defensively.

"Don't waste your time," he said softly. He leaned back in the chair and closed his eyes. He remained that way for a long time.

Julie stared at him, Lorna's words suddenly coming back to her. When she had told her boss about the crying sounds, Lorna had suggested that perhaps Forest was responsible and the whole thing was an attempt to drive her away. But as Julie stared at his face, she knew there was no way he was responsible for this. She'd felt his heartbeat racing as fast as her own. He'd been frightened, too.

He didn't look frightened anymore; he merely looked weary, beaten. She fought her impulse to go sit on the floor next to him, to lay her head in his lap, to comfort him by letting him know that in some strange, perverse fashion she cared.

He opened his eyes and sighed. "We might as well go on back to bed. I think it's all over for the night."

He stood up and Julie followed. Frustration gnawed at her, along with a lingering whisper of fear. She followed close behind him as they went up the stairs. She dreaded the moment when he would go into his room and she would be left all alone. "Forest," she said as they stopped in front of his bedroom door. "What do you think the noise was?"

"It wasn't any sonic boom or earthquake." He hesitated a moment. "It was Christopher."

Julie sucked in her breath. Somehow she'd known he was going to say that. She'd thought the same thing herself. But hearing it spoken aloud caused her mind to rebel at the thought of a dead child causing such terror. "That's crazy. Christopher is dead."

Forest's eyes glittered darkly. "Julie, you've heard him crying. Didn't you feel his cold breath on us while we stood on the stairs? It's Christopher, I know it is."

"But...but why is he here? What does he want from us?"

"From me," Forest corrected her. "He wants retribution from me."

"Aren't you afraid?"

He tilted his head thoughtfully. "No. You have to be alive to be afraid, and I've been dead since the day Christopher disappeared."

His words, so empty, again filled with such loneliness and despair, touched a chord deep inside Julie. Without thinking, she reached up and gently stroked the furrow in his brow, allowing her finger to linger, to stroke down the side of his strong face.

She'd meant to comfort him in some way, but instantly knew she brought him no comfort. His eyes flared, and she knew that her touch had whipped up the wild winds of tension that had whirled between them since the night of their kiss, the same wanton winds that had blown through her earlier when he'd come to her room. And as she gazed into the depths of his eyes, she felt that wind blowing hot and wild around her, through her. She knew immediately what the tension was—desire, pure and unadulterated.

He jerked her hand away from his face and pulled her tight against the heat of his bare chest. A faint groan escaped from him as his hands slid over her nightgown, burning her with heat through the silky material. He cupped her buttocks and eased her closer, against the hardness of his arousal.

She gasped at the intimacy and tilted her head back to look at him. His mouth instantly claimed hers in a ravenous kiss. His tongue invaded her, seeking, demanding, refusing to accept anything but total surrender. And without a second of hesitation, she surrendered.

Forest stepped away from her for only a moment, to give her enough time to protest, to stop the craziness of where they were headed. But she didn't want to stop. He could see the heated lust in her eyes, see the pulse that ticked erratically in the hollow of her throat.

He willed her to find the strength to turn away, to run back into the safety of her own bedroom, for he had no strength of his own. He was tired of being strong. He was sick of being alone. He wanted her, but knew he had nothing to give her except his passion, and his soul-sickness.

Run. Get away from me. He tried to mentally communicate this to her, tried to ignore the way the swell of her breasts pressed invitingly against the silk of her gown, the nipples erect as if seeking the heat of his own chest. He tried to ignore that damnable pulse in the hollow of her throat, wanting nothing more than to press his lips against it, taste the sweetness of her skin, sweep his tongue against the heat of her flesh.

She gasped softly, as if able to read his mind. For a moment their gazes locked, and in her eyes he saw the same desire that swept through him, the desire to take, to fill a need, to abandon all common sense.

As he watched her, willing her away from him, she straightened her shoulders and swept past him, into the moonlit, silvery hues of his bedroom. With a curious sense of dread and exhilaration, he followed her.

He paused just inside the doorway, his breath catching painfully in his chest. She stood by the side of his bed, bathed in the moonlight spilling in the window. As he watched, she reached up and pushed the straps of her gown from her shoulders. It slid down the length of her body and pooled like a puddle of milk on the floor, leaving her clad only in a pair of wispy panties. Her breasts gleamed in the moonlight, small but perfectly formed, the dark erect nipples stirring his blood as nothing had in years.

Still he remained unmoving, trapped by his mixed emotions—the heady desire that soared through him and the knowledge that if he took her, he would awaken a need inside that he had denied for years.

"Forest." Even her voice sounded hot to him, throaty with passion, sultry with promise. She moved to lie down on the bed and opened her arms to him, beckoning him to join her in this moment of madness.

In that instant his inertia broke, and with a muttered curse, he tore off his jeans and approached the bed. He hesitated, the edge of the mattress pressing into his thighs, surprised to realize his body was trembling. For a single moment he was gripped with incredible fear. His mouth went dry as he tried to identify the source of his sudden, overwhelming anxiety. He shouldn't be here with her. He didn't deserve her passion.

She rose to her knees and reached for him. She wound her arms around his waist, her hands caressing the broadness of his back. Her breasts pressed intimately against his chest as her mouth found the hollow of his neck. The flick of her tongue against the heat of his throat caused his fear to fade away and be replaced with a frenzied need to possess her.

The fear that had momentarily gripped him was banished beneath the assault of her nearness, her almost-total nakedness. With a groan, he lowered her onto the bed and joined her in the tangle of sheets and moonbeams.

His mouth founds hers, drinking in liquid fire that warmed him through, and he realized it would be easy to drown in this woman. It would be easy to let go of all control and take her quickly, savagely. It would be easy to immerse himself in sating his own hunger. But he didn't want it that way. He didn't want it to be quick. He clung to control, wanting this moment, this night with her, to last forever.

As he kissed her, his hands sought the fullness of her breasts and he rubbed his fingertips across the turgid nipples, felt them swell and become harder at his touch. "Julie. Julie." He whispered her name as his lips left hers. Her skin smelled clean and feminine, like soap and springtime and woman. He wanted to lose himself in her, crawl into her and away from the pain and loss that had been his companion for so long. He wanted to drown himself in her scent, in the silkiness of her skin, in the heat that radiated from her and warmed places inside him that had been cold...so cold for so long.

He moved one hand down the flat of her stomach and cupped his palm against the silky panties. Her damp heat enticed the fire inside him and he pressed his palm against her as she arched to meet his intimate touch. She sighed in pleasure as his fingers crept beneath the nylon material, finding her moist and open.

Her response, her obvious pleasure, fed his own, his need painful as he struggled to maintain control. "Please," she whispered urgently, and he knew she wanted more. Her eyes were glazed and her skin flushed with her response to his touch, but he wasn't ready to complete what they had begun.

"Not yet," he replied, dipping his head forward so his tongue could flick erotically over the tip of one of her breasts. At the same time he swept her panties down past her hips, to a point where she impatiently kicked them the rest of the way off.

As his fingers once again sought her moist heat, her hips rocked against his hand in a sexual rhythm that caused his blood to surge. His fingers slid in and out, his thumb circling the sensitive area and causing her to gasp, to increase her movements against him.

He knew she was climbing to her peak, could feel the tension that built and rippled through her, and he watched her intently, coveting the expression on her face, her violent response to his touch.

She cried out suddenly and stiffened against him, her body trembling uncontrollably with the force of her climax, and as she melted beneath him, his own control snapped.

He moved on top of her and buried himself in her, gasping as she enveloped him in hot velvet. Then he was lost—lost in the need he'd suppressed for far too long. Lost in Julie.

Julie was lost as well. She had been from the moment she'd stepped into his room, smelled the scent of him that lingered on the sheets, permeated the very air. He surrounded her, his heart beating against hers as he moved inside her. She responded to him in mindless wonder. He filled her as she'd never been filled before, demanded that she meet his thrusts with matching ones of her own.

Somewhere in the back of her mind she knew their lovemaking had absolutely nothing to do with love and everything to do with need. And it was more than a physical need. As he stroked deep within her, he captured her face with his hands, commanding her to look at him, connecting with her in a way that had little to do with what their bodies were experiencing.

She felt his need, shimmering in the air around them, shining from his eyes, which glowed silvery in the moonlight. She felt it echoing inside her and pulled his head down so their lips could meet in a kiss of hunger, of rapture.

And then she couldn't think anymore. She could only feel . . . accept . . . and surrender to Forest.

When it was over, he rolled off her so that no part of his body touched hers. She felt his physical distance, but not as acutely as she felt his emotional withdrawal. She leaned up on one elbow and stared at him, searching for words to bridge the distance between them.

He had one arm flung across his eyes, his expression hidden from her. The moonlight caressed his body, and the sight of his masculinity, the memory of what they'd just shared, stirred desire once again. She fought the impulse to reach out and stroke him, watch as arousal overtook him, force him again to take her to the heights where he'd just swept her.

"Forest?"

He didn't answer, didn't move.

"Forest?" She placed a hand on his arm and felt him flinch beneath her touch. "That was...beautiful." She smiled, realizing how inadequate words were to describe what they'd just shared. He didn't answer, didn't move. "Forest? Don't you think we should talk about what just happened?"

He moved his arm away from his face and looked at her. His eyes glittered dark and hard. "No, I don't think we should talk about it. I think you should go back to your room and forget this ever happened."

"I can't do that." She leaned closer to him, watching as shadows overtook his eyes, shadows that had been momentarily banished while they'd made love. "I don't want to forget what went on between us." She placed her hand on his chest and felt the thundering of his heart. "I want to do it again." She leaned over and flicked the tip of her tongue across his flat male nipple. She was shameless and she knew it, reveled in it. "I want to do it again right now."

His eyes flared, the pupils dilating, and with a thick groan he pulled her on top of him. This time the need, the urgency was gone, but the hunger was still there. And this time it was she who caressed, who stroked, tormenting him until he cried out hoarsely, his harsh face revealing all the emotions he normally guarded so closely.

"Damn you," he whispered as she stroked him to full arousal.

"Yes," she answered heatedly. "Damn me." She'd rather have his damnation than his cool disdain. She'd rather have his anger than the unnatural facade he presented to the world. She wanted to break through the shield he'd placed around himself for the past ten years, shatter it and find the heart of the man.

She hovered over him, her hands touching, lingering, caressing, and her lips did the same. And with each touch, each caress, he cursed her passionately, and she reveled in his rich emotion.

With a low moan that vibrated deep in his chest, he rolled over, taking her with him and placing her beneath him once again. As he buried himself in her she lost all rational thought and allowed herself to be swept to the place he took her, a place of mystery and magic and the exquisite wonder of Forest.

Silence. Again. Only this time they remained entangled, too exhausted to pull away from each other. Time passed, minutes expanded. She matched her breathing to his, relaxing in the slow, steady rhythm.

The moon had moved behind the clouds, casting the bedroom in darkness. Julie didn't think, was afraid to. She didn't have the energy to deal with the regret she knew would come with the dawn. She didn't want to analyze what force, what winds of fate had brought them to this place at this time. She wanted only to savor the sensations that still coursed through her, to relish the state of utter fulfillment that embodied her. With a sigh, she closed her eyes and allowed herself to fall into a dreamless sleep.

CHAPTER NINE

Forest knew the instant sleep claimed her. He felt the energy leave Julie's body and knew she'd given herself up to him completely, trusting him enough to fall asleep.

There had been very little tenderness between them. Their lovemaking had been primal, fueled by need and executed with lust. Only now, while she slept, did he allow his heart to feel what his body had experienced.

It had been so breathtaking to accept what was offered freely, and to respond in kind. She had given not only with her body, but with her heart as well. She'd held nothing back from him and he'd found a soul-soothing magic in her arms. If only it could be this way always. If only the demons that raged inside him could be soothed so easily. If only...

This should never have happened. He'd been a fool to allow Julie and her son into this house, an even bigger fool to allow her into his bed. He'd sworn to himself that he'd never let anyone get close to him again. He would never put another person in jeopardy by allowing himself to care. He couldn't afford to care for Julie, and he definitely couldn't allow her to care about him. He didn't deserve that. He was the worst kind of person...a murderer who'd killed a child he loved.

He eased himself up and away from her and went to the window, where he stood and stared out at the woods. It was a more-profound, deeper-black area in the darkness of the night, but he'd looked out so often he could easily imagine every tree, every twisted vine.

Christopher! his heart cried out. The name brought with it such pain that it twisted his gut. He knew with certainty that the forces that filled this house—the cold spots, the booming, the child's eerie wailing—were all his nephew demanding a pound of flesh from the man who had taken his life. Unfortunately, he couldn't appease him when he didn't know exactly what it was the spirit wanted. Did Christopher want him dead? Was that the only way to give his restless soul the peace it needed? He ripped a hand through his hair and leaned his forehead against the windowpane. "What do you want from me?" he whispered. He couldn't undo what had been done so long ago. Hell, he couldn't even remember what had been done.

Julie. His heart cried out a second time. Damn him for the weakness that had allowed him to make love to her. He couldn't care again. He couldn't take the chance of loving her. He was afraid—afraid of what he was capable of, afraid of what he might do during one of the blackouts that had already ruined his life and stolen the life of another. He had to get her away from here. He had to force them to leave. He had to get them to go before another blackout occurred, before another tragedy happened.

He stood at the window for hours. Dawn was just starting to creep over the tops of the trees when he heard Julie stir. He turned and watched her. The golden morning hues glimmered in through the window and found her, painting her sweet skin with a luminous glow. Her eyes were still closed and he could see her lashes, thick and gold tipped. The bed sheets were twisted around her waist and hips, exposing her breasts and the tantalizing length of her shapely legs.

He was surprised to feel desire rocket through him once again. And the desire brought with it anger—anger at himself for wanting her and anger at her for wanting him. He grabbed his jeans and pulled them on, then moved to the side of the bed and touched her shoulder, ignoring the satin texture beneath his fingers.

"Julie." He spoke her name harshly, needing his anger to guard him, to keep her away.

Her eyelids fluttered, then opened. As she looked up at him, a soft smile curved her lips. It was the smile of a woman sated, heavy with slumber and filled with promise. It was an arrow through his heart, a piercing pain of dreams lost and hope abandoned.

Her smile slowly faded when she saw his expression. She frowned and sat up, reaching for the sheet, as if it would provide shelter from his hard gaze.

"The sun's coming up. You should go back to your own room." He heard the coldness in his voice, and she must have felt it, for she pulled the sheet more closely around her.

She frowned and shoved her hair away from her face, obviously fighting off the last lingering vestige of sleep. "Forest ... I ... don't you think we need to talk about what happened?"

"There's nothing to talk about. It was a stupid mistake."

"Perhaps," she agreed. "But it happened, and I think it fulfilled a need we both had."

He looked at her in surprise, unsure what he'd expected from her. Certainly not this. "Strictly physical," he added.

She hesitated, as if she was going to contradict him, then nodded grudgingly. "Okay, if that's what you need to think."

For some reason her answer made his anger rise once again. He saw only acceptance in her eyes, an acceptance of him that was threatening because he wanted it so badly and knew he didn't deserve it. He deserved her loathing, her hatred. He needed it to preserve the barrier that would keep her safe from the murderer he feared resided within.

He leaned toward her, close enough to see the golden specks that flamed in her brown eyes. "Actually, you're right." He reached out a finger and stroked the side of her cheek, noting how she unconsciously leaned toward his touch. "I did have a need ... an incredible need." He cupped her face in his hands. "I had an incredible need to make love to Jeffrey's wife."

She drew in a sharp breath and jerked away. "You don't mean that," she said faintly, her eyes staring into his as if trying to see into his soul. "That's a despicable thing to say."

He shrugged, noting how the spark in her eyes had intensified, how her lips quivered. His intentional cruelty had wounded her, but he couldn't stop now. He must push her away. "You want to talk about what happened? That's what happened. That's what pulled me to you from the moment you arrived on my doorstep. Jeffrey tormented me from the time I was born. He took from me every chance he got. And even though he's dead now, I'm not finished taking from him."

She stumbled from the bed and grabbed her nightgown from the floor. Her jerky movements were uncoordinated and she gasped for air like somebody who'd been punched in the stomach. He hardened his heart against the tears that glimmered in her eyes as she faced him once again. "I don't believe you," she said, her chest heaving. "This had nothing to do with Jeffrey. There weren't three of us in that bed, there was only you and me."

He narrowed his eyes and swept them down her body, slowly, insolently. "I have to admit, once things got started, I forgot exactly why I wanted you. You're a good lover, Julie. Jeffrey was a very lucky man."

He watched the anger build inside her. It flushed her cheeks a becoming pink and caused her spine to stiffen regally. God, she was beautiful, and her anger fed his desire as intensely as her earlier eagerness had done. "You lied to me before," she said, her voice quivering slightly. "Just a little while ago you told me you weren't afraid of the ghost of Christopher because you were dead, and dead men don't feel fear." Her entire body now trembled with the force of her anger. "You aren't dead, Forest. I know, because dead men aren't bastards." Without waiting for his reply, she turned and left the room.

Forest released a deep sigh and turned back to stare out the window. She was right; he was a bastard. The worse kind of bastard. The bleak emptiness was back, surrounding him, engulfing him. She was right: he wasn't dead. He hurt too damned much to be a dead man.

"I'm out of here," Lorna said at two o'clock the next Friday afternoon. "I've got a couple of leads to check out on a hot new story, then I'm heading home to get ready for my date with Martin." She handed Julie a couple of sheets of paper. "If you could just type these up for me, then you can go ahead on home."

"Sure, no problem," Julie agreed, then added with a sly grin, "Hmm, that makes two weeks in a row you've gone out with Martin. Getting serious?"

Lorna laughed. "It's still a bit too early to tell. I like the way he looks in and out of his jeans, and he makes a terrific homemade pizza, but marriage is not based on sex and food alone. Time will tell if he has other attributes that make him marriage material." She headed for the front door. "Don't forget to lock up," she said, then disappeared into the afternoon sunshine.

It took Julie only a few minutes to type up the letters Lorna had left, then she locked the front door and went into the back room. She'd been waiting all week for an opportunity to look through the old newspapers and see what had been written at the time of Christopher's disappearance.

She quickly discovered that there didn't seem to be any discernible order to the way the papers were filed. As she worked, looking for the time period she wanted, her thoughts whizzed through the events of the past week.

The few times she and Forest had run into each other, they'd circled each other like two wary animals. She was still incredibly angry with him, but oddly enough, her anger was tempered with sadness. She didn't believe the horrible things he'd said to her after they had made love. There was no way she would ever believe that the only reason he had wanted her was because she had been Jeffrey's wife.

She'd felt the loneliness inside him, a deep, abiding loneliness that had reached out to her, and despite his assessment that what they'd shared had been strictly physical, she knew it had been much more than that. She'd felt his soul reaching out, stroking hers. His body had made love to her, and no matter how he tried to deny it, his heart had, too.

More than ever she was determined to find out exactly what had happened on the day Christopher disappeared. No matter how often and how loudly Forest announced his guilt regarding his nephew's death, she simply couldn't believe it. She'd lain in his arms, felt his heart beating next to hers, felt the torment that encased his soul. He wasn't a murderer; he couldn't be. A man who was capable of murder wouldn't be capable of evoking such emotion in her. Something didn't ring true about Christopher's disappearance.

She was determined to discover the truth of what had happened ten years ago, determined to break the bonds of self-hatred that kept Forest an emotional prisoner. As long as he believed he'd murdered Christopher, his heart would forever be encased in ice.

She focused her attention on the task at hand, moving to a second file cabinet when the first didn't yield what she sought.

It was nearly five o'clock when she finally found what she'd been looking for. She pulled out an old, yellowed newspaper with a headline that read Kingsdon Heir Disappears.

Unfolding the fragile paper, she spread it out on the floor, then sat down cross-legged and stared at the photographs on the front page. There were two, one of Jeffrey and Forest, the other a snapshot of Christopher.

She studied the picture of the two half brothers first. It had apparently been taken long before the death of Christopher. The body language of the two men displayed the subtle animosity between them. Jeffrey commanded attention first, looking young and arrogant in the center of the frame. Forest was a step behind him, his body turned slightly away, as if he hadn't particularly wanted to be in the picture in the first place. Julie's heart ached for the young men, whose lives had been torn apart, their happiness destroyed, by the disappearance of a little boy.

She turned her attention to the photo of Christopher, vaguely surprised at his likeness to Bobby. Christopher had the same hair, the same lively dark eyes. Even the shape of their faces proclaimed them to be related by more than mere boyhood.

She scanned the article quickly, disappointed to discover that it told no more than what she already knew—sketchy facts that neither confirmed Forest's guilt nor vindicated him. Looking at the picture of Christopher once again, she sighed and traced a fingertip over the yellowed paper. "What happened to you?"

She leaned back against one of the file cabinets, her thoughts whirling in her head. Was it possible to hate somebody so much you would kill his child? Was it possible for hate to be so intense it could override all love?

In truth, she didn't know. Hatred had never had any place in her life. But she knew it was an emotion that twisted people's guts, perverted their souls, transformed them into monsters. Newspapers were filled with stories of normal, rational people shoved over the edge by hatred.

She didn't believe Forest had killed Christopher. She couldn't believe it. Even in sleep his social conscience surely wouldn't have allowed him to take the life of another. The story Forest had told her simply didn't wash.

She sighed again, refolded the newspaper and placed it back in the file where she'd gotten it. No questions had been answered. Looking at several more papers, she found several follow-up stories, but no new information, no answers to her questions.

As she remembered the fearsome banging that had resounded through the house on the night she and

Forest had made love, a shiver raced up her spine. Had it been what Forest said it was? Had the ghost of Christopher Kingsdon made the walls vibrate and sound like they were falling down? If he was a ghost, then he was a very angry one. Why else would he be haunting the house, unless it was to avenge his death...and demand retribution from the man who had murdered him?

Julie screamed as a loud booming suddenly resounded. Then she shook her head ruefully as she realized somebody was pounding on the door of the office. Leaving the back room, she hurried toward the door, where a petite, white-haired woman was using her tiny fist as a battering ram.

"It's about time," she said, bristling as Julie unlocked and opened the door.

"I'm sorry, we're closed for the day," Julie explained.

"News don't just happen between nine and five on weekdays." The old woman swept past Julie regally and planted herself in the chair in front of her desk. She motioned Julie into the opposite chair. "Well, park yourself if you want a story better than who grew the latest fruit in the shape of some historical figure."

Julie hid a smile as she sat down. She had a strong feeling she knew who sat across from her. "What kind of story do you have for me, Mrs. Windslow?" She ventured the guess and was awarded a wide smile displaying ill-fitting dentures.

Edith Windslow leaned forward, her vivid blue eyes sparking with ancient mysteries and perhaps a tinge of dementia. "You've heard of those encounters of the third kind? Well, I've had better than that." She frowned. "You'd better get paper and pencil ready. You young people don't have memories the length of my nose. Me, I remember everything that's happened in this town for the last eighty years." Her frown deepened and she tilted her head quizzically. "Memory is a perverse sort of thing, ain't it? I can remember what my mama served for my fifth birthday party, but I don't remember what I had this morning for breakfast." She waved her hands, her frown disappearing.

For the next twenty minutes, Julie listened to Edith's latest tale of alien abduction. What the woman lacked in facts, she more than made up for in creativity. Julie dutifully took notes. Even though she knew Lorna would never use the story, she didn't want to hurt Edith's feelings, and in truth found her story fascinating. Besides, the old woman seemed harmless enough despite her wild imagination.

"I know most folks think I'm nuts," Edith said as she rose from the chair at the end of her tale. "But there are some of us who are more in touch with the other side of reality." She hesitated at the door and tilted her head, and her keen blue eyes seemed to peer into Julie. "You know what I'm talking about. You've been touched by the other side, haven't you?"

"No, I don't know what you're talking about." Julie took a step backward, away from the suddenly insightful gleam in the old woman's eyes. What had appeared as dementia before now seemed to be aged wisdom.

"Sure you do. The scent of the spirit world clings to

you.'' Edith reached out a bony hand and placed it on Julie's arm. Her touch was cold and caused a shiver to creep up Julie's spine. ''You have a son, don't you?''

Fear clutched at Julie. ''Yes,'' she answered hesitantly.

Edith closed her eyes for a moment, her head nodding as if she were receiving a secret communication. Her eyes snapped open again, wide and startled. ''Watch him. Guard your boy closely.'' The old woman snatched her hand away, as if having contact with Julie's skin was somehow abhorrent. ''Danger. Danger.'' The madness was back in the bright blue eyes.

She nodded curtly to Julie, then turned and hurried down the sidewalk, muttering under her breath as her head bobbed up and down.

Bobby. The name reverberated through Julie with a sense of urgency. She looked down at her wristwatch and gasped. It was nearly six o'clock. She had never been this late. Julie had arranged her hours so that she would always be home by four, when the school bus dropped Bobby off at the house.

Grabbing her purse, she quickly locked up and ran for her car. As she drove, she fought the panic that threatened. Had Lottie already left for the day? Was Bobby all alone with Forest?

''Forest would never harm Bobby,'' she said aloud, as if speaking the words would make them so. Whatever had happened ten years ago was a tragic accident. Forest couldn't have killed Christopher and he would never do anything to hurt Bobby.

Still, as she remembered the way Forest had looked when she'd stumbled upon him in the woods, fear constricted her throat. No, Forest would never harm Bobby if he was in his right mind. But what if he didn't know what he was doing? What if he had been in the same strange state she'd seen him in in the woods, and had led little Christopher out of the house and killed him?

"Stop it. Just stop it," she commanded herself firmly as she stepped on the gas. She was allowing the ramblings of an old woman to affect her mind. After all, Edith declared that she was whisked away to martianland every Friday night. What did she know about anything?

Still, she had known Julie had a son. She'd known about Bobby, and she'd said he was in danger. The car skidded to a stop before the house, and Julie flew out and through the front door. "Bobby?" she yelled. She paused in the entry hall, listening for a reply. "Bobby? Are you here?" When there still was no answer, she hurried into the kitchen. Empty. No sign of Lottie. No sign of Bobby.

Her heart pounded with such intensity that her chest ached. She left the kitchen and took the stairs two at a time. She raced into her bedroom, then into the smaller, attached room. Bobby's schoolbag was on his bed, his good slacks tossed on the floor. So he'd come home from school and changed clothes. Where was he? Dear God, where could he be?

She gazed out the window, staring toward the woods, afraid she would see Forest leading Bobby down the path toward the dark center of the tangled growth. More frightening was the possibility of seeing Forest walking out of the woods...alone. Her hand covered her mouth in horror at the very thought. Would the crime of ten years ago be reenacted now, with Bobby the innocent victim? Did Forest have a dark side, one he didn't know about, one that thrived on hatred and murder? Oh, God, would Bobby just disappear, as Christopher had done?

Then she saw them. Together. Not on the path that led to the woods, but rather on the patio below her. Forest was helping Bobby to flip hamburgers on a small gas grill.

She leaned her forehead against the windowpane and expelled a small sob of relief. Oh, God, for a moment she had thought...she had feared... Shame flooded through her. She'd allowed a silly old woman to stir horrid thoughts about a man her heart told her was innocent. Was her belief in Forest so fragile?

She watched Forest and Bobby, waiting for her pulse to regain its normal rhythm, waiting for the lingering fear inside her to recede. As she stood there, Lottie bustled out of the kitchen and set a large bowl on the wrought-iron table. She must have been out back when Julie came in a few minutes earlier.

Julie released another sigh, her gaze captured once again by Forest and Bobby. They could easily be mistaken for father and son. Their hair shone with the same dark, rich highlights, and both could use a visit to the local barbershop. If she were closer she'd see that their eyes were shaped the same, although she knew her son's would never reveal the dark torture that deepened Forest's.

At that moment Bobby looked up and caught sight of her. A huge grin lit his face and he gestured for her to come down. She nodded and waved back at him. Her hand froze in the air as Forest looked up, and their gazes locked. Everything she had tried not to think about, tried not to remember since the night they had made love, was there in the heat of his eyes. Unfortunately, the taste of fear still lingered in her mouth like the aftermath of a bad dream. It reminded her that he was an enigma, a man whose inner darkness taunted her with whispers of danger. She wanted so desperately to believe him innocent, but there was a little bit of doubt there, one that had exploded inside her when she'd thought Bobby might be alone with him.

She turned away from the window and quickly changed clothes, then went down to join the people on the patio—the two men closest to her heart.

"I don't know who thought of it, but eating outside was a fine idea," Julie said an hour later as she and Forest sat on the patio. For a change, dinner had been pleasant. It was as if she and Forest had silently agreed to a truce. The tension that had been so thick, so uncomfortable between them since the night of their lovemaking was momentarily put aside. They'd finished eating, and Lottie had whisked the plates away, then left for the night. Bobby was on the back lawn, tossing a football up in the air, then catching it.

"It was Bobby's idea," Forest said. "Actually, he wanted a picnic on the grass, but he agreed to compromise and eat outside. There won't be many more warm evenings.''

''Hmm, all I know is it feels nice to be outside.''

Forest nodded and looked over at Bobby, his expression rather wistful. ''I should take pity on him and play a little catch with him. A football was meant to be thrown back and forth.''

''Why don't you?'' Julie urged. ''I'm sure he'd love it.''

He hesitated another moment, then bounded out of the chair and ran across the yard toward Bobby. Within minutes the two were playing catch. Julie relaxed in her chair and watched them as the evening shadows deepened.

There was something wonderful about watching them play together. As Forest chased after Bobby's errant passes, stretched to catch the ones he could, he displayed a natural athletic ability and grace and reawakened in Julie the desire she had spent the last week tamping down. He was so breathtakingly masculine, and just looking at him made her feel so distinctly feminine. She pushed away these disturbing thoughts, not wanting to dwell on the splendor of being held in his strong arms.

Forest was infinitely patient with Bobby, cheering him when he threw a good pass, encouraging him to work harder when he didn't.

The first time Forest laughed out loud a thrill raced through Julie. She'd never seen him laugh before, had never heard the rich tones, watched his eyes crinkle in merriment. It was beautiful, bewitching, magically transforming his features with inner illumination.

It's not fair, she thought sadly. It wasn't fair that Forest needed the joy of having a child in his life, and Bobby needed the role model of a man in his, yet fate had conspired to make it impossible for the two to give to each other.

This moment together, sharing, bonding, was an anomaly, one Forest would not allow to be repeated. As long as he believed himself to be a murderer, he would forever keep himself isolated, allowing her only a painful glimpse of what might have been.

"Whew, that kid has some energy," Forest exclaimed as he rejoined her at the table. He picked up his glass of tea and took a long, deep swallow.

Never had he looked so attractive to Julie as now, with a sheen of sweat across his brow and a flush of color on his cheeks. She wanted to see him laugh again. She wanted to make love to him again. She averted her gaze and looked back at her son, who was once again tossing the ball up in the air and catching it.

"He's a good kid," Forest said softly.

"You like children," Julie observed.

He hesitated a moment, then nodded. "I never had any interest in children or having a family until Christopher was born." He smiled softly, and again Julie caught a glimpse of the man Forest might have been if tragedy hadn't permanently scarred his soul. "Oh, I suppose someplace in the back of my mind I assumed that, when the time was right, I'd get married and have kids. But Christopher made it all seem so much more real, so much more desirable. I wanted to fill this house with children's laughter." He gazed up at the structure that loomed behind them. "It's never been filled with much of anything but hatred."

"It's not too late," Julie said. "You could still fill the house with love, with children."

He shook his head, and it was as if the dark shadows of the evening emanated from his eyes. "You still don't get it, do you, Julie?" He stood up. "I don't have children ... I kill them."

CHAPTER TEN

"Bobby, it's time to head inside," Julie called as the purple hues of dusk deepened and spread fingers of darkness around them. The night brought with it a cool breeze that rustled the last leaves on the trees and reminded her that winter was just around the corner.

Would she and Bobby still be here when the snow flew? Lorna had told her that winters here could be harsh, with frigid temperatures and deep snow. But surely the winter chill could not compete with the chill Forest's parting words had placed around her heart.

He didn't have children, he killed them. His pronouncement, so stark, so blatant had shocked her. Was she a fool to remain here in this house with a man who believed himself guilty of a heinous crime? If she truly thought Forest was a threat to Bobby's safety, then no financial crisis would keep her here. If she had to, she would live in her car along the side of the road to keep Bobby safe.

But her heart simply refused to believe in Forest's guilt. She realized that watching Forest play catch with Bobby, seeing his features free from guilt and bathed in the glow of happiness, had caused the last of her doubts to fade away. She knew he was innocent as surely as if she'd been there on that day, as if she actually knew what events had led up to Christopher's disappearance. Forest was not a killer, and she was gambling her life and her son's on her gut instinct.

Still, she hadn't been there and she didn't know exactly what had happened. Forest had said he'd fallen asleep, had insisted he'd killed in his sleep. But that couldn't possibly ring true. Something else had happened that day, something he hadn't told her.

All she had to do was figure out why he felt so adamant about his own guilt. He'd fallen asleep; the child had wandered off and gotten lost. It was probably as simple, as tragic as that. So why on earth did he believe he'd done something terrible? What secret did he hold? What else had happened that day that made him so certain of his own guilt?

She rubbed her forehead tiredly, aware that the night was growing colder. ''Bobby, come on now. It's getting too cool and dark for us to be out here.'' She stood up and looked across the yard to where Bobby appeared to be talking to himself. He had his hands on his hips, and although she was too far away to hear what he was saying, his face was twisted in a frown. It looks like Bobby and his imaginary friend are having a fallout, she thought.

She frowned, wondering if she should be worried about the appearance of this new imaginary friend. Surely not. Surely it was just a harmless manifestation of a lonely little boy.

Once he was more adjusted in school, and as he made more plans with his new friends, this newest imagined playmate would just disappear, like Gifford the Rabbit had years ago.

"Bobby," she called again, the tone of her voice letting him know she was losing patience.

"I'm coming," he yelled. He picked up his football and ran toward her. As he drew closer, she could see his troubled expression.

"Honey, is anything wrong?" she asked.

"Nah, my friend just doesn't want me to go inside yet. He's mad at me."

Julie smiled. "Perhaps your friend doesn't catch colds as easily as you." She met him at the edge of the patio and threw an arm around his shoulder. "Besides, the nice things about imaginary friends are that they don't stay mad for long."

"But he's not...oh, never mind." Bobby's foot caught on one of the concrete patio bricks, displacing it and nearly tumbling him on his face. He regained his balance and leaned down to replace the brick, but paused. "Hey, Mom, there's something down here." He reached down into the space the errant brick had revealed and withdrew a small, metal strongbox. "Wow, I wonder what it is. Maybe it's a treasure chest. Pirate's gold or something cool like that."

Curious, Julie took the box from him. "Come on, let's go inside and see what you found."

They went into the kitchen. Bobby danced around the table with excitement as Julie tried to decide if they should open the box or take it directly to Forest. When she saw the initials etched in the metal, however, she knew she wasn't going to fetch Forest, at least not until she'd looked inside.

Whatever the box held would only add to his pain. With one finger she traced the indented letters *CK*.

Christopher Kingsdon. Besides, perhaps there was a clue of some kind inside, a clue to what had happened to the little boy. "Come on, Mom. Open it," Bobby encouraged eagerly.

"Yes, yes, all right." Julie fought down a slight tinge of guilt as she unhooked the latch and opened the box. Inside there was no pirate's gold, no splendid treasure, but something even more valuable. Polished rocks, a tattered bird's nest, old photographs, a rabbit's foot—the treasures of boyhood all safely preserved in a metal box. Her heart ached as she thought of the little boy who had tucked these treasures inside, a little boy who had met a mysterious, tragic end.

"Wow, who do you think this all belonged to?" Bobby asked curiously. He took the white rabbit's foot and rubbed its furry softness against his cheek.

"I'm not sure," Julie answered. She wasn't ready to talk to Bobby about Christopher, although eventually she knew she would have to tell him about his half brother. Still, she knew right now he would only find it confusing to discover that his daddy had had another wife, another son, a full life before he'd been in their lives. "Maybe we should just give this to Uncle Forest," she finally said. "He'll know what to do with it."

Bobby replaced the rabbit's foot with a sigh. "I wish it would have been pirate's gold. That would have been so cool."

"It's time you wished yourself right up into a bath. Go on," she said, stilling the protest she knew was coming.

"If I was a pirate I'd never have to take a bath," Bobby grumbled as he left the room.

Julie sat down at the table and pulled one of the photos out of the box. It was a picture of Forest and Christopher. The little boy was no older than three, and his arms were wrapped tightly around Forest's neck. Forest looked so young, with no torment, no torture in his eyes. There was such joy, such love emanating from their faces that it was like a knife twisting in Julie's heart.

It was time she talked to him again. When he'd told her about Christopher's disappearance, she'd had the suspicion he was holding something back...that there was a piece of evidence or something he'd refused to divulge. It was time she pressed him.

She looked at the picture once again and realized why she was so determined to prove Forest innocent. The stakes were suddenly enormously high. She was falling in love with him.

"Oh, no," she gasped softly as she allowed the full intensity of this new discovery to sweep through her. She hadn't intended this to happen, had fought against it since the moment she'd arrived. But somehow, some way, Forest had managed to touch her in a place she felt had never been touched before...right in the center of her heart.

She could stop it all now—stuff the feelings she had for Forest into the darkest recesses of her mind and not allow them to go any further, not allow them full bloom. If he never touched her again, if she refused to allow the memories of their lovemaking to enter her thoughts, then perhaps the crazy feelings would pass like a painful, but harmless case of the flu.

She stood up and relatched the catch on the box, wishing she could lock her emotions away as easily. As it was, she knew she would have to lock them into her heart and not allow them any escape. There was no hope here. There was no future with a man like Forest. He was tainted with the bitter relics of his tortured past, condemned to spend his life alone…in the rancor of his own self-hatred.

Realizing Bobby was probably finished with his bath, she took the box and went upstairs. Later, after he was tucked in bed for the night, she would give the box to Forest. After all, it wasn't right for her to keep these pieces of Christopher from him. She wasn't in the position to make a decision like that.

It was nearly two hours later that Julie finally got Bobby into bed and worked up the nerve to go down to the workshop, where she assumed Forest had been since he'd left them in the backyard.

She crept down the stairs to the basement, reluctance slowing her pace, the box tucked under one arm. She could hear him in his room, the sounds of sandpaper rubbing against wood. She hesitated outside the door, realizing this place had become his sanctuary. This was his asylum from the town, where his exalted position as mill owner made him not quite belong. From a past he couldn't forget and an offense he couldn't forgive.

Julie knocked on the door, trying not to remember that the last time she'd been inside the workroom they'd shared an explosive kiss that had rocked her very senses. She tried to forget that she now carried a part of his painful past under her arm.

He opened the door. "Something wrong?" he asked curtly. He moved back across the room and sat down at the bench. He picked up a figurine and began sanding it once again, not looking at her.

"No. Nothing's wrong. I'm sorry to bother you...." She felt a flush heat her face as he paused in his work and gazed at her.

"You've done nothing but bother me since the minute you arrived here." For a moment he looked at her objectively, as if he had successfully removed himself from her, as if she was nothing but a stranger who had mistakenly wandered in here.

Her flush intensified. She would have to work very hard to achieve the same detachment. "That was never my intention," she said softly. She moved closer to where he sat, her attention caught by the figurine he was working on. "Oh, that's beautiful." She took another step nearer, to see more clearly the wooden bird Forest held.

"It's a falcon," he said softly. "Do you really like it?"

The bird's wings were bent in midstroke, giving an immediate impression of flight, of freedom. The hooked beak gave the raptor a proud nobility. It looked beautifully savage, like the man who had crafted it. She nodded in answer to his question.

He looked at the bird dispassionately. "Did you know that falcons are often trained to kill crows?"

She shook her head, unsure what he was talking about. He gave one wing a final brush with the sandpaper, then held it out to her. "It's finished. You can have it."

"Oh, no, I couldn't...." And yet her hand reached out, as if of its own volition. When she took it, she was still able to feel the warmth of his hand in the wood. She held it for a long moment, then set it down on the table, suddenly remembering why she had come down here in the first place. "I have something for you." She took the box from beneath her arm.

His eyes widened, first with recognition, then with pain. "Where did you get that?" His voice was husky, filled with the emotions he normally kept so tightly capped. He reached out a hand, then withdrew it, as if both drawn and repelled at the same time.

"Bobby tripped over one of the bricks in the patio. This was hidden underneath it."

Forest inhaled deeply, then took the box from her. His hands trembled slightly as he ran his fingertips across the etched initials. "I gave this to him when he was five. He was such a collector of stuff and always had things shoved in his pockets. We decided he needed a treasure chest, a special place to store all the good stuff a boy could find."

He placed the box before him on the worktable and stared at it, as it afraid to open it up, see what remnants of Christopher lay within. "I etched his initials here on the morning of his fifth birthday."

Julie moved to stand directly behind him, knowing how difficult this would be, wanting to comfort him but not knowing how. She felt the tension rolling off him in waves and wondered how many times in the last ten years he had faced painful relics of the past alone.

She watched as he opened the box. A small, almost inaudible groan escaped him as he began to pull out the items one by one, holding each for a long moment, then laying it aside. Julie placed a hand on his shoulder, needing to connect with him, wanting him to know she shared his pain.

He gasped softly as he withdrew a heart-shaped ruby from the very bottom of the box. He held it up and shook his head ruefully.

"That's from Lottie's necklace," Julie exclaimed, remembering when the housekeeper had told her about it.

He nodded, holding it so that the bright light overhead danced in the cut of the stone. "That little scamp. I always suspected Christopher had found this someplace around the house and had kept it. I used to call him the Little Crow. From the time he was a baby he loved bright, sparkly things." His hand closed around the jewel, clutching it so tightly his knuckles turned white.

"Forest?" Julie spoke softly.

He spun around on the stool and caught her by the waist, pressing his head against her heart. Although his face was turned into her, so she couldn't see his expression, she felt the sobs that suddenly ripped through his body, and she held him tightly. She stroked his hair, trying to absorb some of his pain, make it more manageable for him.

And as she held him, she realized she couldn't ignore her feelings for him. She couldn't avoid what her heart told her—that she was helplessly, irrevocably in love with Forest Kingsdon. And as the utter hopelessness of that love swept through her, she held him closer and allowed her own silent tears to fall.

She didn't know how long she remained there with Forest's tears staining her blouse and her own tracking, one after another, down her face.

Finally, the sobs that had racked his body diminished, then stopped altogether. Still he held on to her waist, as if she was his only salvation, and she held him, too, wishing she could be his redemption.

With a low moan, he finally released his hold on her and sat up. Julie's heart ached at the emptiness revealed in his face. He looked as if all he'd had inside were tears, and with them gone, he had nothing left within.

"Please," he said, turning his face away from her, obviously embarrassed. "Please...just get out. Leave me alone. I need to be alone."

"Forest, you've had the last ten years to deal with this alone. Isn't that long enough?"

He looked up at her, his eyes black as night and as empty as death. "Christopher is gone forever, and that's how long I'll be dealing with what I've done. Now, please, leave me." He turned back around and buried his head in his arms. The overhead light caused the ruby heart beside him to glitter as if mocking her, mocking her love.

Again hopelessness overwhelmed her. The past had an unyielding hold on Forest, a hold she didn't know how to break. She couldn't fight the spirit of a little ghost boy, couldn't break the bonds that would keep Forest captive forever.

She picked up the wooden falcon, then turned and walked out of the room, granting Forest his wish to be alone. Climbing the stairs slowly, she felt her heart ache with her newly discovered love, a love doomed by the mysterious events that had happened ten years ago. Never had she felt so helpless, and her helplessness stirred an anger at the Fates who had cast her here, with another man incapable of love.

"What do you want from him?" she whispered as she walked through the living room. "Let him go, Christopher." She talked to the walls, to the ceiling, feeling foolish and yet compelled to beg a spirit to release his possessive hold on the man she loved.

Climbing the stairs to her room, she felt old, ancient, beaten by things she didn't understand, couldn't comprehend. She knew there was an enormous capacity for love in Forest, a capacity he refused to entertain because of the crime he thought he'd committed. As long as he believed he'd murdered Christopher, he would never allow himself to reach out to her or anyone else. He would forever refuse to seek happiness.

She sat down on the edge of her bed, overwhelmed by the hopelessness that seemed to permeate the very walls of the house. Sighing, she quickly changed into her nightgown, then peeked into Bobby's room to check on him before retiring herself.

Moonlight spilling in the window showed that Bobby's bed was empty. "Bobby?" She turned on the light to make sure her eyes weren't deceiving her. He was nowhere in the room.

The bathroom, she thought immediately. Quickly she went down the hall, the first niggle of worry sweeping over her as she realized the bathroom was dark and empty. "Bobby?" She ran down the hallway to the second bathroom. It, too, was empty. The fear that had only been a whisper inside her now exploded. Where was Bobby? He'd been in bed, sound asleep, when she'd gone downstairs to talk to Forest, but that had been almost an hour ago. He almost never got up in the middle of the night for anything. Where had he gone? Where could he be?

She pounded down the stairs, her heart thundering erratically as she remembered the odd look in Edith Windslow's eyes. "Danger. Danger," the old woman had said when she'd spoken of Bobby. And now the feeling of imminent danger was horribly real.

"Don't panic," Julie warned herself. Maybe he was in the kitchen getting a late-night snack. That thought reassured her as she raced toward the kitchen. Bobby wasn't there... but the back door was wide open, letting in the cold night air. She hurried to the door and peered out. The moon was brilliant overhead, sending down a luminous light that painted the landscape in ghostly fashion. Toward the back of the yard, heading toward the woods, was her son.

His pale blue pajamas shone starkly in the moon's glow, silhouetting him against the deeper darkness of the looming woods. For just a moment those very woods seemed to breathe, seethe as if with a life force of their own. The thick grove of trees appeared to move with ominous intent, and she imagined she could feel a nearly imperceptible pull directed at her son.

"Bobby!" she screamed, terrified at the sight of him heading toward the black growth of the woods. His feet stopped and he hesitated. "Bobby," she yelled again, and he turned to look in her direction.

The cold night air surrounded her as she stepped out the door. "Bobby, get in here," she cried, her fear mingling with the first stirring of anger. What on earth was he doing outside at this time of night? He knew better. She'd often told him of the dangers of wandering in the woods. She was vaguely aware of Forest's footsteps hurrying up the stairs from the basement.

"What's going on?" he asked, coming to stand behind her. "What's he doing out there?"

"That's what I intend to find out," Julie replied, not taking her eyes off her son. He was still turned toward her, but he wasn't moving. It was as if he was torn, trying to decide whether to follow whatever impulse had led him out into the darkness of the night, or listen to his mother, who called him back.

Again Bobby turned and looked toward the woods, his body poised as if to run away from his mother, away from safety.

"What in the hell is he doing?" Forest asked tersely.

Julie didn't know if the fear that surrounded her was her own or Forest's. All she knew was that her body thrummed with a pulsating rhythm of imminent tragedy.

"Doesn't he know it's dangerous out there in the dark?" Forest said angrily. "I'll go get him." He shouldered his way past her, but at that moment, whatever had kept Bobby stationary snapped, and he ran toward Julie and Forest.

When he reached them, Julie grabbed him by the shoulders, her fear momentarily displaced by anger. "What on earth are you doing out here?" she asked. Hysteria rose up inside her and she fought against it. "I should spank the living daylights out of you."

Bobby's eyes were huge as he gazed first at his mother, then at Forest. "I'm sorry, but I had to, Mom. I had to come out here. He wanted me to, and I couldn't make him mad."

"What are you talking about?" Julie asked. Without waiting for an answer, she led him back into the warmth of the house, aware that his little body was quivering with a chill.

She didn't say another word until she had him in front of the fire in the living room, where the warmth of the flames effectively battled the chilliness of the night.

Forest walked over to the bar and held up a bottle of brandy. When Julie shook her head, he poured himself a glass and sat down in his wing chair.

"Now, talk to me, Bobby. You've been told time and time again not to go near those woods, yet here you are in the dark of night heading right toward them." Julie's shiver dispelled the worst of her terror.

Bobby sat down on the floor, refusing to meet her gaze. "I knew you'd be mad. I told him you'd be really mad. But I couldn't help it. I told you, he wanted me to go. He told me I had to."

"Who, Bobby?" Forest asked. "Who told you to go out into the woods?"

"My new friend," Bobby answered, then looked defiantly at his mother. "And he's not imaginary. He's as real as me, and he's magic."

"Oh, Bobby." Julie sighed in frustration. "You're old enough to know the difference between what's real and what's imagined, and you know that you're never supposed to go into the woods. Now I don't want to hear any more nonsense about this new friend."

Bobby stood up, his little face twisted with his own frustration. "Mom, he's real! He's as real as you and me! He wanted me to go into the woods, and I couldn't help it. He made me go. He made me do it!" Tears spilled down Bobby's face. "He's as real as I am, and he's got dark hair like me and his name is Christopher... Christopher the Crow."

Bobby sobbed and ran from the room just as Forest gasped and stood up. His brandy glass fell from his hands, shattering against the hardwood floor, and his gaze sought Julie's. Terror drenched her once more as the implication of what Bobby had said swept through her. It wasn't an imaginary friend that had called him into the woods in the middle of the night. It had been the ghost of a dead boy.

CHAPTER ELEVEN

For a long moment neither Forest nor Julie spoke. The air around them vibrated with the lingering aftermath of Bobby's shocking words. The fire snapped, shooting sparks that caused Julie to jump. Forest bent down to pick up the shards of his broken glass.

Julie watched as he moved with wooden footsteps to the bar, where he grabbed a towel, then cleaned up the last of the mess from the dropped glass of brandy. It was impossible! Her mind rebelled with protests as she replayed Bobby's words in her head. And yet she knew it wasn't impossible, and the thought that a dead little boy was communicating with her son filled her with a kind of horror she'd never before experienced.

When he finished cleaning up the mess on the floor, Forest stood up and met her gaze. "Julie, there has to be a logical explanation," he protested. She knew he was wrestling with the same doubts that assailed her. "Surely Bobby heard us talking about Christopher and borrowed the name for his imaginary friend."

For a moment uncertainty swept through her. Yes, surely that must be the answer, she thought. But it didn't make sense, and she quickly shoved the idea away and shook her head vehemently. "No, Forest. Bobby didn't hear us talking, and his friend isn't imaginary." She should have known it was more than her son's imagination. She'd seen him talking to his "friend," had watched him only that evening in the yard having an argument with him. She should have known it was something more than just a lonely little boy playing let's pretend.

She shivered and wrapped her arms around herself, trying not to remember the terrifying moment when she'd been afraid Bobby would ignore her call and run into the darkness of the woods. She'd felt the magnetic pull emanating from the trees, an otherwordly energy drawing Bobby away from her, away from safety.

"The spirit of Christopher tried to lure him into the woods. Why?" Hysteria rose up inside her once more. "Why, Forest?" She moved forward until she stood in front of him, her eyes pleading for answers. "What does he want with Bobby? Dear God, what's going on?" Her voice rose a full octave with the last question, and he grabbed her by the shoulders as if to keep her from falling apart.

"Julie." He said her name sharply, but she barely heard him. All she could hear was Edith Windslow's words of warning: *Danger. Danger.* The old woman had seen Bobby at risk. What did Christopher want with him? Why had he wanted Bobby to go into the woods in the middle of the night? Did Christopher want Bobby dead? Oh, God, did he want her baby dead like him?

Numbly she allowed Forest to lead her to the sofa and pull her down next to him. Her thoughts spun around and around in her head as she tried to separate a little boy's fantasy from reality. Maybe Forest was right, she thought wildly once again. Perhaps Bobby had heard them mention Christopher and had simply borrowed the name for his imaginary friend. Yet even as she thought this, she knew it wasn't true. In an instant, she remembered the chilling air that often filled Bobby's bedroom, the night that the rocking horse had been wildly moving by itself.

Christopher had been in Bobby's room. This wasn't a case of Bobby's imagination; it was a case of a true paranormal occurrence. "Forest, what's happening? What does Christopher want with Bobby?" she asked.

He placed an arm around her shoulder and drew her against his warmth. As she rested there she realized for the first time that she was trembling uncontrollably. "I don't know," he finally answered helplessly. "Are you sure there isn't any way that Bobby might have heard us talking about Christopher?"

"He called him Christopher the Crow. Forest, you told me just this evening that that's what you used to call Christopher. There's just no way Bobby could have heard that or made it up." She shivered again. "I've seen him talking to Christopher. I've felt Christopher's presence in Bobby's bedroom." She pulled out of Forest's embrace and looked at him. "You have to tell me again exactly what happened the day Christopher disappeared. You have to tell me everything."

He looked at her in surprise, his jaw tightening. "But I've already done that," he protested.

She stared at him, seeing once again the haunting secret that always seemed to linger just at the edges of his dark eyes when he spoke about that day. "You have to tell me every detail that you can remember."

He reacted with anger. "What good will that do? I've already told you everything that happened. There's no point in going over it all again."

"You didn't tell me everything, did you?" she asked softly. She looked at him expectantly. He hesitated. "Damn it, Forest, this isn't just about you anymore. This is about Bobby being in danger, and in order to know what we're up against, I need to know the truth . . . the whole truth."

He sighed and raked a hand through his hair, and something seemed to absorb all the light in his eyes. "I told you that I fell asleep and ..and I must have killed him while I was sleeping." She nodded and he exhaled deeply. "That's not the whole truth."

Julie felt a shiver of fear spiral up her spine. She had a sudden desire to place her finger over his mouth, stop him before he said whatever he was about to say. She wasn't at all sure she really wanted to know the whole truth. Then she thought of Bobby, and the fear that had lit his eyes, the horror that had suffused her as he'd walked toward those dark woods. "Then tell me the whole truth. Tell me what happened."

He didn't look at her. Instead he stared into the fireplace, as if his greatest wish was to jump in and let the flames consume him. "I was sleeping, dreaming peaceful dreams, but something woke me." His voice was low, without emotion and she realized he'd once again removed himself far from the events of that tragic day.

"Go on," she said. She placed a hand on his arm and squeezed lightly.

"It was the click of the back door opening that woke me. I knew Christopher must be leaving the house. He loved the woods, and even though he'd been warned many times not to go near them alone, he often went exploring. I remember standing up, intending to stop him before he got out of the house. I reached the back door and looked outside, but he'd already disappeared into the woods. That boy could run like the wind. Anyway, that's when everything went blank. I blacked out."

Julie frowned. "What do you mean, you blacked out?"

He turned and looked at her, his face yielding a helpless horror that caused the fear inside her to intensify. "I remember standing there, and the next thing I knew I stood in the middle of a small clearing in the woods and I could hear a scream, his scream still lingering in my mind." His hand trembled slightly as he rubbed it across his lower jaw. "I knew immediately that something horrible had happened . . . that *I* must have done something horrible. Why else would I be standing in the woods? Why else would Christopher's scream be so loud, so vivid in my mind?"

Julie stared at him. "Had you ever had that kind of blackout before?"

He shook his head. "That was the first time."

"But it wasn't the last," she observed knowingly. He looked at her in shocked surprise. "I saw you, Forest," she admitted. "I saw you when you were in one of those blackouts," she said.

"What are you talking about?" he asked hoarsely.

"You were in the woods. It was—I don't know—
about a week ago." Julie remembered that moment
when she had spied him through the branches. She's
been struck by his slow, almost dreamlike movements, the utter passivity of his face. It all made sense
now. It hadn't been drugs. It had been some kind of a
blackout.

Forest grabbed her hand, his grip almost painfully
tight. "Wha-what was I doing?" he asked.

"Ouch. Forest, you're hurting my hand." He immediately released his hold, but the tension rolled off
him as he leaned toward her, his features twisted with
inner torture. She realized at that moment what Forest's greatest fear was what haunted him day and
night. He was afraid that in a blackout, he turned into
some kind of a monster. "Oh, Forest, you weren't
doing anything." She took his hand once again. "You
looked like a sleepwalker. If that's the state you were
in when Christopher disappeared, you didn't kill him.
You couldn't have."

Oh, God, how he wanted to believe that. He'd been
afraid...so afraid of what happened to him in those
blank moments he experienced from time to time. It
was always the same—the scent of the woods, thick
and oppressive, then nothing. He always came to in
the same clearing, Christopher's favorite place, always in fear of what he'd done.

It wasn't until this very moment that he realized how
much Julie's denials of his guilt soothed his soul, and
he longed to let her hold on to her belief in his innocence, despite his fear to the contrary.

The fact that she hadn't believed he was a killer, refused to accept that he was capable of such an act, had been the first comfort he'd allowed himself in years. But he couldn't allow it. He couldn't let her believe in him. He couldn't let her obscure what he knew: that he'd done something to Christopher, and now Christopher's spirit wanted revenge.

"Julie, you've got to take Bobby and leave here," he said. "I'm afraid for you, for him."

"I don't intend to do anything until I talk to him some more and find out exactly what's been happening with this little friend of his. If it really is the ghost of Christopher talking to him, contacting him, then maybe we can figure out why, what it is that Christopher wants from all of us."

Forest looked at her. "I know what Christopher wants. He wants retribution. He wants me dead, too."

"Have you been to the doctor about your blackouts?" Julie asked, as if she hadn't heard what he'd said.

He nodded. "After that first one, after Christopher disappeared, I thought maybe it had something to do with the accident at the mill, the bang on the head I'd gotten. I went to doctor after doctor, had every test ever created. Nothing." Bitterness rang in his voice, a bitterness he couldn't control as he remembered the tests, the doctors, the futility of seeking answers nobody had. "I went to the best specialists money could buy and they all told me there is absolutely nothing physically wrong with me."

"That's ridiculous," Julie scoffed. "There has to be something that's causing them."

"I even went to a couple of psychiatrists, certain that I was a multiple personality or was just plain insane, but they sent me home, said the fugues were probably stress related or figments of my imagination." He laughed bitterly, then sighed and looked at Julie again. "They didn't think I'm crazy, but I know I am. There's no other explanation for the blackouts, and what I did to Christopher."

"Come on, let's go talk to Bobby." She stood up and took his hand. "Maybe we can find some answers."

"Julie, I was serious. I think you and Bobby should leave here." It suddenly seemed extremely important to him that he know they were safe....out of harm's way, out of the reach of the evil that was happening here. "I'll pay to get you relocated someplace else."

"We'll talk about that later. First we need to talk to Bobby and see what he knows about our angry little ghost."

Forest hesitated, touched by the fact that she simply refused to run away from this house, from him. "Julie, I said I'd pay for you and Bobby to leave here. You can pick wherever you want to live in the whole country."

She shook her head. "I can't leave."

"Why not?" he asked.

She smiled softly. "You told me once that one of my most irritating characteristics was my curiosity, and at the moment it's raging completely out of control. I'm not leaving here until I get some answers." Her smile faded. "Besides, we don't know what Christopher wants with Bobby. It's possible that no matter where we go, no matter how far we run, he'll still haunt my son until he gets it.'' He saw the fear that glimmered in her eyes at this thought, but then it vanished and strength shone through. She held out her hand to him. "Come on, Forest. Maybe together we can make some sort of sense out of all this craziness."

He looked at her hand, stretched toward him. How he wanted to take it, feel the warmth of her support as her fingers clasped his. But no matter what questions still needed to be answered, there remained one irrefutable fact—Christopher was dead and he had been there, had heard the boy's last scream, had probably caused that scream. Ignoring Julie's hand, he stuffed his own in his back pockets and followed her up the stairs.

Bobby was in his room, although he wasn't asleep. His light was on and he lay on his back, as if waiting for them to join him. When they walked in he sat up and looked at his mother anxiously. "Am I still in trouble?" he asked, then caught his lower lip between his teeth.

"No, honey, you aren't in trouble," Julie said, sitting down on the edge of his bed. "But we need to talk about Christopher."

Bobby nodded, glancing at Forest, then back to his mother. "Mom, Christopher isn't imaginary, but he isn't real like me, either."

"What does he say to you?" Forest asked.

Bobby shrugged. "Different stuff. We play together. He likes to play hide-and-seek."

Forest gasped and leaned weakly against the doorframe. He wasn't sure he'd believed it until this very moment, but he knew now with certainty that Bobby was in touch with Christopher. Somehow Christopher had managed to breach the veil that separated the physical plane and the spiritual one. What were Christopher's intentions? What did he want from Bobby? Forest could understand Christopher's haunting of him. He'd always assumed Christopher's cries were intended to drive him over the edge of sanity or into a guilt-induced suicide. So why was Christopher manifesting to Bobby?

"When did you first see him?" Julie asked.

Bobby frowned thoughtfully. "It was right after we moved here. At first I'd just see him standing at the edge of the woods. Then one night he came to my room and talked to me, and we became friends."

"When does he talk to you?" Julie asked.

Bobby shrugged. "Different times. Sometimes he comes during the day, but mostly at night right before I go to sleep. He talked to me in school one time and got me in trouble with the teacher."

Julie looked at Forest, and he knew what she was thinking. If Christopher talked to Bobby in school, that meant the spirit wasn't tied to this house or the woods. It meant it was possible that Christopher might appear to Bobby no matter where they went.

"Bobby, honey, we believe Christopher is the ghost of a little boy who died a long time ago," Julie explained. Forest could see Julie's care in choosing her words and knew she was trying to decide how much to tell her son about his half brother. "He got lost in the woods and died, and we don't know why he's come back. We don't know what he wants."

"I knew he was a ghost," Bobby said. "I knew because he can fly and turn invisible and do all kinds of cool things." The excitement that lightened his voice faded and he frowned once again. "I knew you'd get mad if I went into the woods, but Christopher wanted me to go. He told me I had to, and I couldn't help it."

"Did he say why he wanted you there?" Forest asked.

Bobby shook his head. "No, he just wanted me to go."

"You mustn't go into the woods, ever again," Julie said firmly. "It doesn't matter what Christopher tells you or how much he wants you to. The woods are dangerous, and you must never go there again."

Bobby nodded and yawned sleepily. Julie stood up. "That's enough for tonight. We'll talk more in the morning." She bent over and kissed Bobby goodnight, then she and Forest went back down the stairs and into the living room.

Forest headed directly to the bar and poured himself a second glass of brandy, hoping he could drink this one. He needed it. He needed to warm the chill that had taken up residency deep inside him.

"I'd like one of those, too," Julie said as she sat at the edge of the sofa closest to the fire. Apparently she had an inner chill as well, Forest thought. He carried the drinks over to where she sat and handed her one, then sat down beside her.

As she stared into the fire, he looked at her. The hysteria that had played on her features earlier was gone, replaced by a wrinkled brow that indicated deep thought.

She was clad in the nightgown she'd worn on the night they'd made love. It was a silky, long white gown that emphasized the perfect swell of her breasts and the slender curve of her hips. He was vaguely conscious of her scent, sweet and floral, surrounding him.

She leaned back and the wrinkle in her brow smoothed, as if she was finding a certain peace as she stared into the fire. But under her soft exterior was a will of iron, he knew. She'd survived what he suspected had been a rather unhappy marriage. She'd managed to overcome Jeffrey's tragic death and financial ruin. She was strong, but he had a feeling she was now up against more than she could handle.

He remembered the night they had made love, the feel of her breath against the hollow of his neck, the way her body had yielded to his as if they'd been made specifically to fit together. It was a tantalizing memory, one he'd tried to keep out of his mind, away from his heart since the night it had happened. But now he allowed the memory to play through him, rich and full, every nuance of it an exquisite torture.

He could love her if he let himself, but he couldn't allow himself that luxury. He still didn't know what happened to him in his blackouts. He still didn't know what he was capable of during one of them.

He frowned as he remembered the harsh words he'd said to her on that night they'd made love. The hurt that had radiated from her eyes haunted him as effectively as did Christopher's mournful sobs. "Julie?"

She turned and looked at him, her gaze soft, accepting. He stared into his brandy, unable to look at her and speak of that night without revealing the fact that he wanted her again. And he didn't want to complicate things between them.

"Forest, what is it?" she asked softly.

"I just wanted to apologize for the things I said to you . . . those things about Jeffrey. What we did was a mistake, but what I said to you afterward was unforgivable."

Her fingers touched his arm, then reached up and stroked the side of his face. Fire. Her touch was like fire against his skin, evoking the familiar heat of desire inside. It was a fire that burned twofold, lighting the flames of passion and burning him with the fact that he couldn't accept the warmth. He grabbed her hand and removed it from his face.

"Julie, you and Bobby should leave here, leave me." He forced himself to look at her. "It isn't safe for you any longer. You have to face the fact that there's no way to fight Christopher. He wants revenge against me, and perhaps what he's doing is using Bobby to get to me. There's danger here." He stood up angrily. "And there's no guarantee that I'm harmless. There's no guarantee that in one of my blackouts I won't take Bobby out in those woods and make *him* disappear."

She took a sip of her brandy and set it down on the coffee table, then stood up and approached him. "Forest, somehow, some way we're going to figure this all out. At least Christopher is talking to Bobby. Perhaps we can communicate with him through my son. We can find out exactly what happened the day he disappeared, and we can find out why he's still here, haunting this house, these woods."

Forest opened his mouth to protest, to tell her that he knew why Christopher was doing what he was, but she placed a finger against his lips. "Forest, there's no guarantee that Christopher won't continue to communicate with Bobby no matter how far we run. You heard what Bobby said—that he's come to him in school. That means he has the power to manifest outside this house and the place where he died."

She removed her finger from his lips, the strength he loved back in her eyes. "This has become our home, and I'm not about to let the ghost of a seven-year-old run me out." She reached up and touched her lips to his. "I'm going to bed now, and tomorrow maybe we can figure out how to give Christopher whatever he needs to finally rest in peace." She looked at him for another long moment. "Perhaps we can find a way to finally give you the peace you need."

For a moment, as she gazed into his eyes, he saw the reflection of the man he would have been without this tragedy. He saw the man she thought him to be, and the vision, the need to be that man, ached inside him. She touched his face one last time, then turned and left the room.

Forest sank down on the sofa. The taste of Julie's lips still lingered on his mouth. Her scent remained in the air, rich and intoxicating. How easy it would be to open his heart entirely to her. She was so sure of his innocence, and that certainty was a balm to his soul. Unfortunately, it was a belief he couldn't share.

Peace. Oh, God, if he could only find peace. He knew what Christopher wanted. He wanted revenge, retribution; he wanted Forest dead. And before Forest would allow himself to harm Bobby, or allow Christopher to harm either Julie or her son, he would grant Christopher his wish. If he had to, he'd kill himself first.

CHAPTER TWELVE

Julie was already up and in the kitchen when Forest came down the next morning. He looked at her in surprise. "What are you doing up so early?" he asked.

"Waiting for you." She smiled and gestured toward a chair at the table, then poured him a cup of coffee and set it before him.

"Where's Lottie?" he asked, looking at his watch. "She's usually here by now."

"She's already been and gone. I sent her home," she said and his dark eyebrows lifted quizzically. "She took Bobby to spend the day at her house as a favor to me."

"Why?"

Julie drew in a deep breath, unsure how Forest would react to her next words. "Because I didn't want to have to worry about Bobby while you and I go ghost hunting."

"Ghost hunting? What are you talking about?" He stared at her blankly. "I've got to go to work."

"The mill can't run for a day without you?"

He frowned. "Well, I suppose it could, but..."

"Call in sick." She hurried on before he could protest. "Forest, I thought about this all night long. Maybe the reason Christopher is talking to Bobby is because Bobby is a child and open to the experience. I'm sure it never occurred to Bobby to fight against Christopher's spirit. His childish innocence, his untainted mind allowed the communication to happen.''

''So what does that have to do with my going to the mill today?''

''I just thought that maybe you and I could go into the woods, into that clearing where you awoke after your blackout on the day Christopher disappeared. Maybe if we open ourselves up, call to Christopher, he'll come and talk to us.'' She flushed at his obvious skepticism. ''I know it sounds crazy, but do you have any better ideas?''

''Only one.'' He looked at her, his eyes dark and foreboding.

''What?'' Julie asked, a strange apprehension sending cold fingers up her spine. ''Forest, what are you talking about?'' There was something in his tone, a glint in his eyes that somehow frightened her.

He shook his head. ''Never mind. I'll call the mill and tell them I won't be in today.'' He stood up, then hesitated, his hand on the wall phone. ''We'll try it your way first.''

''And then?'' Julie asked, still apprehensive. What was he thinking? What dark thoughts flitted in his mind and caused his eyes to blacken in despair?

He shrugged. Instead of answering her question, he turned, picked up the phone and dialed the mill. As he spoke to one of the foremen, Julie went to the window that provided a view of the woods.

She took a sip of her coffee, her gaze lingering on the spot where Bobby had stood in the darkness the night before. Why had Christopher called him there? Why did he want him to go into the woods? The question had kept her awake most of the night. Was Forest right? Was the ghost avenging itself on Forest through Bobby? Anything could have happened to Bobby out there in the darkness. He might have gotten lost; he could have been hurt. He might have died...was that what Christopher wanted? She shivered and took another sip of the hot coffee.

She looked back at Forest. She'd sat through the wee hours of the night, holding the wooden falcon that Forest had given to her, and she'd realized her love for him was all tangled up with her unshakable belief in his innocence. There was no way to separate the two. She loved him, and that love refused to accept the possibility of his guilt. But if he hadn't killed his nephew, then why had Christopher come back? Why was he haunting them?

Forest's blackouts frightened her because she didn't know what they implied. What caused his loss of consciousness? If there was no medical basis for the condition, then what? Did he suffer some sort of mental aberration?

Forest hung up the telephone and turned back to Julie. "Okay, I'm free for a day of spirit hunting."

"You have to take this seriously or it won't work," Julie exclaimed, then added, "although it might not work anyway." She sighed. "All I know is I refuse to just sit idly by and be terrorized by a ghost child." She looked at him and her eyes flashed defiantly. "And I still refuse to believe that you killed that little boy."

"And I keep telling you that I believe I did," he answered dully.

For a long moment they simply looked at each other. She knew her unshakable belief in him shone from her eyes just as strongly as his agonizing doubt gleamed from his. "I guess all we can hope for is that Christopher will be able to tell us which one of us is right."

He nodded curtly. "You'd better get a jacket. It will be cool in the woods." He grabbed a denim jacket that hung from a hook just inside the back door. "We might as well get this show on the road."

"Forest, it is worth a try, isn't it?" Her gaze searched his face, loving the strength of his jaw, the shadowy depths of his eyes.

He hesitated, then nodded slowly. "At this point I'm willing to try anything to finally discover some answers." His voice was weary. "This has to end, Julie. I'm tired of living like I have for the last ten years. I'm tired of the guilt. One way or another this all has to come to an end soon."

Again apprehension snaked up her spine at the resigned tone of his voice. Where before he'd always exhibited self-loathing and a crippling guilt, sometime in the last couple of weeks he'd moved beyond that, she realized, into a weary kind of acceptance that for some reason scared her.

"Forest, it will be all right," she said softly. She went to get her coat from upstairs.

Forest turned and stared out the window where Julie had stood while he'd spoken on the phone. The sky above was gray. It was as if the sun knew what journey he and Julie were about to take and hid in fear of their dabbling into the spirit world of ghosts. It was a crazy idea, but at this point he was willing to try anything. He sensed danger moving closer, not only to him, but to Julie and Bobby as well. There was a strange sort of energy, like an electrical current resonating in the air. He had the feeling that somehow psychic energy was gathering, gaining strength and substance for some malevolent reason.

"Ready," she said from behind him.

He turned to see her bundled in a cranberry jacket, which managed to match the color of her cheeks. For a moment he felt breathless from her beauty. Wildly, irrationally, he fought the impulse to grab her up and whisk her far away from this house. However, he knew no matter how far they ran, no matter what distance they traveled, they couldn't escape the madness they'd been dealing with...for he feared that madness was inside himself.

"Julie." He took her by the shoulders, his hands caressing the cotton jacket beneath his fingertips. "Before we leave here, before we go out into those woods, you have to promise me something."

"What?" Her eyes searched his, the tone of his voice apparently frightening her. Good; he wanted her frightened. He needed her frightened to assure her safety. "If we get into the woods and I feel a blackout coming on, I'll tell you to run. Do it. Don't wait, don't

question me. Run like the devil himself is after you."
For he just might be, Forest thought to himself.

"Forest, I'm not afraid of you."

He tightened his hold on her shoulders. "You have to promise me, or I won't go. You should be afraid of me. I'm afraid, and besides, I couldn't live with another... another accident..." His voice trailed off.

She placed the palms of her hands on either side of his face, her eyes gazing into his. "Okay, I promise."

He relaxed, realizing belatedly how tense he'd been, how frightened he'd been of going into the woods alone with her. "Okay, then let's go."

Together they went out the back door and into the crisp morning air. "Looks like rain," Julie observed, glancing up at the overcast skies.

"Perfect haunting weather," Forest said with a wry smile.

Julie gazed at him thoughtfully, her stride matching his as they walked across the overgrown yard. "I wish I had known you before." She flushed slightly and looked down at the ground.

"Why?"

She looked at him again, her eyes so clear, so devoid of guile. "Every once in a while you exhibit just the hint of a wonderful sense of humor."

Forest nodded and breathed in deeply. "It's been a very long time since I've found anything remotely humorous." He looked up at the overcast sky, then back at her. "I lost my sense of humor the day Christopher disappeared." He focused his attention on the woods they were approaching. He'd lost his soul on that day so long ago. *Oh, Christopher, I'm sorry. Whatever*

part I played in this...I didn't mean it. I loved you.
Forest felt the anguish, the despair that was never very far from the surface rising up inside him as the tangled growth and dense trees drew closer and closer.

Julie sensed the darkness rising up inside him. She saw his features grow tense, the muscle in his jaw jump and clench ominously. It was as if the shadowy aura of the woods suddenly grew within him, muffling his light.

They didn't speak as they entered the woods and followed the path Julie had taken on the evening she'd seen Forest in his odd state of fugue. She walked behind him, wishing for sunshine to banish the deep shadows that filled the narrow path. She stifled a squeal as some unseen animal scurried away from them, rustling dead leaves as it ran to safety. Forest turned and looked at her, his eyes as black as night. "Okay?"

She nodded and wrapped her arms around herself, as if her own embrace could bring her comfort. He turned and continued walking. She wanted to spin around, run back to the house. She hadn't quite anticipated the oppressive quality in the air. She wasn't ready for the ominous shadows, the scent of death that hid in the thicket surrounding them. She hadn't expected Forest's absolute withdrawal into himself and whatever darkness resided inside him.

Maybe she was wrong about him. Maybe her belief in his innocence was only the naiveté of a woman blinded by love. She'd seen women like that on television talk shows, women in love with mass murderers, blinded to the evil by their sick love. Maybe he really did have a dark side, one she had never seen, but one that had reared up on a day long ago and had culminated in the death of a little boy.

Maybe that dark side was only released out here, in the woods where there were no laws or social mores, where nature was at its most wild and savagery was the only rule. Panic knotted in her chest, a raw panic that made breathing difficult, almost impossible. Her eyes widened as he suddenly spun around again to face her, his eyes black orbs that radiated no light, no hint of his inner thoughts.

"Julie." His voice was hoarse and he held out his hand to her. In that instant Julie realized that it was grief that blackened his eyes, guilt that twisted his features, and all her doubts faded in the knowledge of her love for him. She took his hand and squeezed it, reassured by his touch. He led her into the same small clearing where she'd seen him before. "This is where I came to consciousness after Christopher disappeared," he said softly. "This is where I heard his last scream."

"This is where I saw you when you were in a blackout," she replied. "Something draws you here, so this is where we'll sit." Julie sank down onto the leaf-covered ground and patted the spot next to her. He sat down and they were immediately surrounded by a thick, heavy silence. Not an insect buzzed, not a single bird called, not a breath of air stirred. It was as if they were in a strange sort of vacuum.

"I've been back to this same clearing a thousand times in the past ten years," he said, breaking the stillness.

"Probably more times than you are aware of," Julie said. "I would guess you come here every time you black out. When I saw you, you were walking back and forth like you were in some sort of a dreamworld. Your face..." She hesitated, unsure how to describe the beauty of his face without his worries darkening his features. "You just looked like you were in a dreamworld," she finished inadequately.

"More like a nightmare," he said starkly.

"Tell me about Jeffrey and you," Julie said.

He shrugged. "What's to tell? We hated each other."

"Always?"

He frowned thoughtfully and stretched out on his side. A leaf clung to his hair and she reached over and picked it off, refusing to allow her fingers to linger in the thick locks she loved. "There was a time I thought the sun rose and set in Jeffrey," he finally said reflectively. "He was my big brother, strong and confident, and more than anything, I wanted us to be friends." He rolled over on his back and folded his arms beneath his head. "But Jeffrey didn't want to be friends. I was a baby when my mother left town and Richard brought me here. From the time I can first remember, Jeffrey was angry at my very presence. I think he hated me because he was afraid that somehow I'd take all our father's love and leave nothing for him. He was accustomed to being alone, being the little king. He was afraid I'd somehow usurp his position."

He closed his eyes, and for a moment Julie wondered if he'd fallen asleep. But his eyelids flickered and she realized he was entertaining memories of his painful past. He opened his eyes suddenly and in them she saw the light of revelation. "I didn't hate him, not really. I—I think I loved him. And in Christopher I got the chance to love him all over again. It was like having Jeffrey without his hate, without his fear. In Christopher I saw all the good that might have been."

Julie smiled, pleased that at least in this, he had found a certain amount of peace. Her smile faded as another thought came to mind. "But Forest, if you really didn't hate Jeffrey, then why would you have killed Christopher?"

The peace he'd momentarily found was fragile and deteriorated beneath the weight of her question. "I don't know," he whispered hopelessly. "Perhaps I really am a monster," he added, closing his eyes once again. He remained that way only a moment, then sat up, anger tugging at his features. "This was a stupid idea," he said irritably. "I can't believe I actually let you talk me into this."

"As I recall, you didn't have any better suggestions," she answered dryly.

"Well, this is stupid," he returned.

"Forest..." Julie sat perfectly still, her heart thudding in a rapid rhythm of expectation. Cold air flowed over her, frigid air that had nothing to do with the weather or lack of sunshine. "Don't you feel it?" she whispered urgently. "He's here. Christopher is here."

Forest tensed. "Julie...run," he said, his teeth clenched tightly together. "Run."

But she couldn't. She couldn't move. Faint, childish sobs drifted over her, penetrated her, evoking tears.

Loneliness and despair overwhelmed her. The crying was eerie, rising and falling on the wind, but there was no wind. Julie felt as if all humanity's suffering was contained within the sobbing, and it pierced her heart, the very depth of her soul.

It was as if she lost all sense of self and knew only the deepest, darkest anguish. It filled her, consumed her, and she sobbed beneath the weight of it.

"Julie, for God's sake," Forest yelled frantically, his face taut with the last vestige of control. "I'm losing it. I'm blacking out. Get out of here! Run!"

The crying stopped at the same moment that Forest's eyes went completely blank and the paralysis that had held Julie captive snapped. She jumped up, poised to run, but hesitated, her attention arrested by Forest.

He stood up, his face completely devoid of emotion, his eyes open but unseeing. He walked slowly, hesitantly back and forth in a small area. He paused occasionally and tilted his head as if listening to some inner voice. He whispered something, a single word so soft she couldn't hear it.

Julie felt no threat of physical danger from him. It was as if his life force had disappeared, or turned so far inward it couldn't be detected. The cold still encircled them, along with a pulsating energy.

She stepped closer to him, needing to hear what word it was he kept repeating over and over. "Forest?" She said his name softly, experimentally, unsure what his reaction would be.

He paused and turned toward her, but she knew he didn't actually see her. Once again he tilted his head. "Five," he whispered.

"Five what?" she asked.

He frowned, as if the question were far too difficult to answer. "Five," he repeated, then the blackout passed. His eyes filled with emotion and instantly she felt his energy once again radiating from him. He sank down to the ground, his body trembling violently.

"You didn't run," he accused harshly.

"I couldn't." She searched his face, which looked achingly weary. "Are you all right?"

He hesitated, then nodded. "Just tired. I'm always exhausted after a blackout." He looked at her again, this time with a touch of fear. "What did I do?"

"Just paced back and forth, and you said one word—*five.*"

"Five?" He frowned. "Why would I say that?"

Julie smiled in frustration. "I was hoping you'd be able to tell me what it means."

He shook his head. "I have no idea."

"Come on, let's go home and warm up."

He stood, and she went to his side to support him. Together they made their way out of the clearing and back to the house. Once inside, they shrugged out of their jackets, and Forest set about making a fire in the living room.

When the flames danced warmly, he and Julie sat down on the floor before them, as if they needed the proximity of the fire to chase away a bone-shivering chill.

Forest stared into the blaze, wishing he could jump into it and put a finish to all this madness. When would it all end? When would Christopher's cries for justice be answered? God, he was tired of living with the burden of his guilt.

"Forest?"

He turned to look at Julie. The fire's glow painted her features in lush golds, and he wanted her, wanted her fire to ease his pain, wanted her energy and passion to surround him. He wanted her to keep him from feeling the hopelessness that had become an all-too-familiar companion. He wanted to reach out to her, to take her in his arms and make love to her. But he couldn't. He wouldn't use her in that way. It wasn't fair. It wasn't right.

"What do you feel just before you black out?" she asked, her brow wrinkled in thought. "You were able to warn me that you were losing it, so you must feel something."

He nodded, gazing back at the fire, unable to look at her without wanting her. "Just before I black out I always smell the woods and feel a horrible cold, and I'm overwhelmed by anguish. Then it happens."

Julie leaned closer to him, so close he could smell her heady fragrance. "Forest, those are the same things I feel when Christopher is present. The cold, the despair...somehow your blackouts and Christopher's spirit have to be tied together."

He sighed. "But that's not possible. I had the first blackout on the day Christopher disappeared." He stared at her, wanting to defuse his need for her. "I killed Christopher in that blackout," he reminded her harshly.

"We don't know that, and I don't believe it," she returned evenly. "Oh, Forest!" She sighed softly and put her arms around him, in what he knew was an attempt to comfort him. But it didn't help. Instead it enticed him, evoking emotion so strong, so intense that he couldn't fight against it, and in truth didn't want to.

He pulled her onto his lap and found her lips, already parted and eager, as if this was what she'd intended all along. He found the fire he'd wanted in her mouth and jumped in, needing it to sweep away his despair, his guilt, the loneliness of his life.

Her mouth gave to him, with nothing held back. Her tongue met his boldly, echoing the hunger that raged inside him. As the kiss continued, his hands crept up beneath the fleece of her sweatshirt, drawn to the warmth of her bare skin.

He pushed her bra up to free her breasts, and she moaned softly into his mouth, further heightening his desire. It took only moments before he was frustrated with the excess material of her clothing. With her help, he pulled the sweatshirt over her head, then removed her bra.

Then it was her turn to help him take off his shirt. Immediately he pressed her against him, loving the friction of her soft breasts against his muscular chest. By mutual consent, with no words spoken, they both stood up and took off their jeans, baring themselves completely to the warmth and light of the fire and each other.

Somewhere in the back of his mind, Forest knew they were about to do what he'd sworn he wouldn't do again. Somewhere in the back of his mind he knew it was wrong—all wrong, for he was a damaged man who had nothing to offer her except this moment in time, this passion so intense.

She stood hesitantly, the glow of the fire playing on the sleek length of her legs, the sweet swell of her breasts, the lovely lines of her face. She didn't cringe at her nakedness, despite the hot gaze he cast on her. Rather, she stood proudly, as if she were a gift to him. And she was—a gift of light, of goodness after too many years of being alone.

He approached her and reached out and caressed her face. She closed her eyes and tilted her head into his hand. He remembered the last time they'd made love. It had been all lust, primal and frenzied. He didn't want that now. He wanted soft sighs and sweet exploration. He wanted to take all the time left in eternity. He wanted forever.

His heart thundered as he reached out to touch the swollen bud of her breast. He realized his anticipation was almost as sweet as actual consummation. He bent his head and flicked his tongue over the pebbly hardness of her nipple. She moaned again and sagged slightly. Together they sank to their knees on the floor, their mouths seeking and finding each other once again.

Julie. His head was filled with her. Julie. His heart overflowed with her. There was no room for any other thought but her. As they kissed, her hands stroked languidly up the muscles of his back, then tangled in the hair at the nape of his neck. Her body moved against his in a sensual dance of tactile pleasure. He could feel the heat of her, smell the feminine scent of desire, and he wanted to drown in her forever.

Her hands worked their way down his back once again, the feather-light caresses sending him spiraling up to a higher plane of desire. A gasp escaped him as her fingers encircled his hardness. Their lips parted and he looked into her eyes, saw the glazed brightness there.

He eased her down onto the rug in front of the fire, the heat of the flames equal to the heat that came from her. "Julie, Julie," he whispered against the sweet hollow of her neck.

She moaned in response as his fingers found the source of her heat, delved into her velvety softness. He watched her face in the fire's glow, coveting the waves of pleasure that swept over her features as his fingers stroked within.

They took turns pleasuring each other with silken strokes, exploring the nuances of passion, finding hidden points of exquisite pleasure as part of their intimate discovery. He marveled in the marbled smoothness of her skin and in the honeyed taste of her. He felt as if he'd known her forever, perhaps in a million lifetimes before. She offered the comfort of an old love, the frenzied excitement of a new one.

When he finally possessed her, easing deep within her, he felt complete, connected as he'd never before been in his life. As she accepted him, opening beneath him like a flower to the sun, moaning his name over and over, he knew this was to be his true torture.

He looked deep into the depths of Julie's eyes and knew the memory of this moment would stay with him long after she and Bobby had moved on, long after she realized there was no future here with him. This he would remember forever. This would be his torment.

As they rode the crest of passion together, he realized that this—the memory of loving Julie—would be the true haunting that would eventually break him.

CHAPTER THIRTEEN

Julie remained in his arms for a long time after they finished making love. Slowly their heartbeats fell into sync, finding the rhythm of complete fulfillment. Still she remained, reluctant to break their union.

It wasn't until she realized he'd fallen asleep that she finally eased up and out of his arms. She grabbed her clothes from the floor and went upstairs. She took a quick shower, redressed, then went back down the stairs to where Forest lay sleeping in front of the fire. She curled up in the chair where he normally sat and watched him.

It was a pleasure to indulge herself in watching him sleep. He looked younger, the lines of his face nearly invisible in repose. She'd wanted to tell him, she'd wanted to speak of her love while they had made love, but she'd been afraid. He'd done very little to make her believe that his feelings for her were anything but desire. He'd never indicated to her in any fashion that he might be falling in love with her.

Still, as she watched him sleep, she allowed her love for him to flood over her, warm her from within. The fire played on his body, casting warm golden hues on his splendid nakedness. He was so beautiful. Surely a man so beautiful couldn't be evil. Shoving this thought aside, she stared at him once again.

She could see the sinful length of his lashes, sooty black against his paler skin, the whisper of whiskers that darkened his lower jaw. The lips that were normally held so tightly, so tautly, were relaxed into a becoming fullness as he breathed softly in and out.

Oh, Forest, she thought wistfully. If only there was some way to ease your torment. If only there was some way to prove to you that you aren't guilty of killing Christopher. If only I had the ability to make you whole again.

She stared into the fire, knowing she wished for the impossible. How could she prove to him something that she couldn't even prove to herself? Her belief in his innocence was simply a gut instinct.

She straightened in the chair as Forest stirred, looking like an awakening golden giant as he stretched and eased himself up to a sitting position. "What time is it?" he asked, still groggy with sleep.

"Not late. You didn't sleep very long."

He raked a hand through his tousled hair, then looked at her for a long moment.

She tensed. "Please don't say it," she begged softly.

"Don't say what?" He frowned and stood up. He scanned the floor, spying his jeans, then grabbed them and pulled them on.

"Please don't tell me it was all a mistake." She couldn't stand it if he said that.

He sank down on the sofa and ran a hand across his jaw, then sighed. "No, I won't tell you that," he finally said. "I can only tell you that this is all there is.

Julie, I have nothing to offer you. No promise of a future, no promise of tomorrow."

"I'm not asking you for any promises," she said evenly, although her heart wanted more, cried out for more.

He closed his eyes, as if pained by her words. "If you refuse to leave here, if you intend to continue to live in this house, there is something you have to promise me." The torment was back on his face, wild and savage as he gazed at her.

"What?" she asked. At this moment she was almost willing to promise him anything.

"You have to promise me that you will never allow Bobby to be alone with me. Never."

"Forest . . . I—"

"Promise me," he thundered angrily.

"I promise," she instantly agreed, wondering at his intensity.

"It's a promise you cannot break," he added, then slumped back against the cushions of the sofa, his eyes closed once again.

"Forest?" She was frightened, not so much by him as for him. She moved from the chair to the sofa and sat down next to him. "Forest, what is it?" She searched his face. "Talk to me. Tell me what you're thinking."

"I don't know." He rubbed his jaw, then looked at her once again. "I just feel like things are reaching a crisis. Can't you sense it in the air? An energy, a horrible kind of pressure?"

"I . . . yes, I feel it," she admitted reluctantly. She'd hoped it was just her. She'd hoped the pressure, the heavy anxiety, was just her imagination.

"What if it's inside me? What if it's me who's about to explode? God, I'm so frightened for you and Bobby." His eyes seemed like soulless, dark orbs. "If I killed Christopher, then there's no guarantee that I won't kill again, and Bobby is the most vulnerable." His gaze turned hard. "You have to make certain he's never alone with me in the house."

She took his hand and held it tightly, wishing she could sweep his fears away, but knowing she couldn't. All they could do was wait and see what Christopher had in store for them. "I promise," she said, knowing that, in at least this, she could offer him some comfort. "I promise," she repeated, and leaned her head against his thigh.

Bobby changed out of his clothes and into his pajamas. He was pooped. At first, when his mother had wakened him early and told him he was going to spend the day with Lottie, he'd been upset. Lottie was old, and even though she was nice, he didn't want to spend his whole Saturday with her. But he could tell his mom was in no mood for him to argue with her, so he'd gone with Lottie.

But surprisingly, it had been a fun day. Lottie had taken him to her little house, and the first thing she'd done was fix him the best cinnamon rolls he'd ever tasted in his life. He'd eaten four, then she had talked him into helping her rake leaves in her yard.

They'd spent the afternoon at the movie theater, eating hot, buttered popcorn and licorice sticks. Bobby decided if he could choose a grandma, he'd pick somebody like Lottie, who laughed at all the funny spots and didn't hide her eyes when the movie was bloody.

After that he'd helped Lottie cook supper, and she'd entertained him with stories about when his dad and his uncle Forest were little. All in all, it had been a surprisingly good day.

"Bobby?" His mom knocked on the door, then came into the bedroom. "All ready for me to tuck you in?"

He nodded and climbed beneath the sheets. As his head hit the pillow, he yawned tiredly. His mom smiled and sat down on the edge of the mattress. "Tired?" she asked.

"Yeah. Lottie might be old, but she wore me out."

His mom laughed. "I have a feeling Lottie could wear out anyone," she said.

Bobby nodded thoughtfully. "Mom?"

"What, honey?"

"Do you think it would be okay if I sort of pretended that she's my grandmother?" He looked at his mother to see her reaction.

For a moment she didn't answer, then she smiled— one of the smiles that told him she was happy. "I think Lottie would be proud if you wanted to pretend she's your grandmother." She leaned forward and kissed him soundly on his forehead. "Now, my little man, it's time to close your eyes and go to sleep."

"'Night, mom," he said as she rose from the bed and turned off his light.

"Good night, Bobby," she said, then left the room.

Almost immediately Bobby felt the coldness that always signaled his friend's arrival. He remained still, knowing that Christopher would show himself when he was ready. He could smell the odor of the woods, as if his room were suddenly filled with trees and brush and mossy rocks. He grinned in anticipation.

Hi.

Bobby sat up and instantly saw Christopher sitting on the back of the large rocking horse. He wore the same jeans and sweatshirt that he always wore, and the horse creaked and groaned beneath his weight. "Hi, yourself," Bobby replied.

Where were you all day? I was lonely.

"I spent the day with Lottie," Bobby answered. "We went to the movies." He smiled shyly. "I wish you could have gone with us."

I don't like it when you leave here.

Bobby shrugged. "I had to go. My mom made me."

Let's play a game.

"Sure," Bobby agreed enthusiastically. "What do you want to play?"

Let's play hide-and-seek.

Bobby frowned. "We can't play hide-and-seek in here. The room is too small. There aren't enough places to hide."

Let's go outside and play. There's lots of places to hide out there.

Bobby shook his head vehemently. "I can't. I got in trouble last time I went out to play with you."

But you have to. I want to play and you're my friend. You're my only friend in the whole world.

Bobby hesitated. It was nice to have a friend that would come to his bedroom at night. He didn't want to make Christopher mad, but he didn't want to make his mom mad again, either. He shook his head. "I'm sorry, I can't, Christopher. I'd probably get a real good spanking if I go outside. My mom was really mad at me the last time I went outside in the dark."

Christopher rocked the horse faster, the smile fading into a petulant frown. *I thought you were my friend.*

"I am your friend," Bobby protested. He wrapped his arms around himself, aware that the room was growing colder. A weird pressure was affecting his eardrums—that and an unpleasant humming sound.

If you're really my friend, you'll come with me outside. Come to the woods with me, Bobby. Please. I need you to come with me.

Bobby hesitated, and in that instant Christopher disappeared. Bobby scrambled from the bed and looked out the window. The night was black, but standing at the edge of the woods was Christopher. His form shimmered, as if he had swallowed the moon, and he raised a hand, beckoning for Bobby to come with him.

Come on, Bobby. The desire to follow Christopher was nearly overwhelming. Bobby felt Christopher's need, intense and almost physically painful. He wanted to go with him, but his mother's warnings about the danger of the woods rang in his ears.

"No," Bobby whispered fervently. He climbed back into bed and pressed his palms against his ears, frightened as he felt Christopher's rage sweep over him. Cold...it was so cold. "Don't be mad, Christopher. I can't," he whispered, squeezing his eyes shut.

After tucking Bobby safely into bed, Julie went downstairs and found Forest in the kitchen, fixing himself a sandwich of leftover ham from their evening meal. "Want one?" he asked.

She shook her head and sat down at the table. "Bobby must have had a wonderful day today with Lottie. He asked me if he could pretend that she's his grandmother."

Forest grabbed his sandwich and joined her at the table, a smile curving the corners of his mouth. "Lottie would be thrilled by that. She should have married and had a dozen kids and grandkids of her own."

"She never married?"

Forest shook his head. "She has a sister, but other than that, we were always her family." He leaned back in the chair. "Lottie was as near a mother to me as anyone," he said reflectively. "My father's love was conditional, but Lottie's was always there, no matter what." He took a bite of his sandwich and chewed thoughtfully. "Even though she thought there was a possibility that I might have done something terrible to Christopher, she never stopped caring about me."

"I guess that's what family is supposed to do...believe in you even when the odds aren't in your favor."

He smiled ruefully. "Not the Kingsdon family. There was never any doubt in Jeffrey's mind that I was guilty."

Julie felt his pain as swiftly, as sharply as if it were her own. "When tragedy happens, people always look for somebody to blame. You were the most convenient scapegoat. That doesn't mean Jeffrey was right."

Forest's smile faded. "I just wish I knew what I could do to give Christopher peace."

And I wish I could give you some peace, Julie thought. Before she could speak, the lights overhead flickered off, then on again. "Ah, speaking of the devil," Forest said softly when the lights flickered once again.

"Forest!" As the lights went off and stayed off, Julie sought his hand across the expanse of the table. Before she could find it, however, his fingers closed securely around her wrist. The darkness of the kitchen was impenetrable. "Forest?" she whispered as he pulled her up from the table. His grip was tight as he led her toward the back door.

She heard the click of the door opening, felt a cold breeze sweep over her face, smelled the night air reaching out for her. She tried to break loose from his grasp, afraid as he pulled her closer and closer to the doorway. "Forest, what—what are you doing? Where are we going?" She planted her feet, his hand pulling her with incredible force.

At that moment a glow lit up the doorway between the kitchen and the living room. She turned and saw Forest across the room, standing there with a candle in his hand. Whose hand . . . whose hand was holding hers? In the dim illumination of the candle glow she looked down and saw nothing . . . nothing around her wrist. She emitted a single scream, then sank to the floor in a dead faint.

When she came to she was lying on the sofa and the lights were back on. Forest hovered over her, his face gaunt with worry. "Are you all right?" he asked anxiously as she slowly eased herself into a sitting position. She winced and gripped the side of her head, which palpitated like a bass drum. "You hit your head on the floor when you fainted. Are you sure you're all right?"

She nodded, her fingers examining the side of her head, where a lump was forming. "How long was I out?"

"Only a minute or two. Here, put this on your head." He handed her a damp washcloth. She did as he said, holding the cool cloth against her brow. She sighed as the pain ebbed to a dull throb.

"Julie, I didn't mean to frighten you," he said apologetically. "As soon as the lights went out I went into the living room to get a candle."

She shivered. "And while you were gone, somebody took my hand and pulled me toward the back door. I—I thought it was you. Then I saw you and—" She broke off and stared down at her hand. "It was Christopher. He wanted me to go outside, into the woods."

Before Forest could answer, the lights flickered off, then on, and once again the air grew cold. "He's coming again!" Julie exclaimed. She stood up and reached for Forest. He grabbed her, held her tightly against the length of him. Then the lights went out and the booming began.

"Mommy!" Bobby's terrified cry came from upstairs and shot through Julie like a fierce electrical shock. Not Bobby, she prayed. Don't hurt Bobby.

"Bobby!" she yelled back, and together she and Forest ran up the stairs. She sobbed as they stumbled and her shin banged painfully into one of the steps. Forest helped her up and they hurried on. "Bobby!" she screamed again, her fear for her son racing through her. They met him in the hallway. He lunged into them in the darkness.

"He's mad," Bobby sobbed. He burrowed his head against Julie's midsection. "He's mad 'cause I won't go with him outside."

"It's all right," she said, hugging him tightly against her as Forest embraced them both. "It's all right," she repeated mindlessly. The three of them stood together in the hall as the house around them exploded in sound.

Boom. Boom. Boom. Boom. Boom. Silence. Then the same. Over and over again it came, always the same pattern. Five, Julie thought. Five. That's what Forest had said while he was in his trancelike state. Five. She wanted to tell Forest. It was important. Christopher was trying to tell them something. But she couldn't compete with the noise that surrounded them, and so she clung to Bobby, clung to Forest and waited for Christopher to finish his tantrum.

"But what does it mean?" Forest asked, his voice harsh with frustration.

"I don't know," Julie answered softly, not wanting to waken Bobby, who slept on the sofa nearby. She and Forest sat on the floor in front of the fireplace, trying to figure out what it was Christopher was trying to tell them. "Five," she repeated. "It has to mean something. First you said it when you were in your blackout, then the booms came in series of five. He's trying to tell us something, but what does it mean?" She shivered and picked up the poker to stir the embers of the dying fire.

"Here, let me." Forest added another log, then took the poker from her.

Julie frowned thoughtfully. "What is he trying to tell us? I should have gone with him when he was pulling me outside."

The poker hit the floor and Forest grabbed her by the shoulders, his eyes blazing as hotly as the flames. "Don't be a fool. You can't trust him. He might have been luring you to your death."

"But he's just a little boy," she gasped softly.

"A dead little boy." Forest released her shoulders and picked up the poker once again, his gaze fixed on the fire. "If I killed him and he wants revenge, the greatest pain he could cause me would be to harm you and Bobby."

It was the closest he'd ever come to admitting that he cared about them, and Julie cherished the words. She hugged her knees to her chest and stared into the fire. The house itself still radiated a strained sense of expectation, as if it was holding its breath, waiting for the next explosion of spirit energy.

Julie shivered, wondering what the next occurrence would bring. There was no way to prepare, no way to defend against this kind of intruder. Locked doors, closed windows—nothing worked against an apparition who wanted inside. "So, what do we do now?"

Forest put the poker away. "I guess we wait and hope that somehow Christopher will let us know what he wants, hope that we figure out what 'five' means."

"He's getting bolder, more desperate." Julie shivered again as she remembered that moment in the kitchen when she'd felt that hand wrapped around her wrist. It had felt so real and had pulled her toward the door with such intent. "What we need here is an official Ghostbuster," she said.

He smiled tightly. "I checked the yellow pages. Unfortunately, the town of Kingsdon seems to be curiously lacking that particular kind of business establishment."

"Hmm, too bad." She grinned. "Maybe when this is all over we could start a business. Kingsdon and Kingsdon, Ghostbusters Are Us. Let us clean your house of all unwanted ghosts and goblins." She giggled, knowing her punchy mood was due to a mixture of exhaustion and stress, but unable to stifle it.

Forest grinned, too, as if her laughter were infectious. She clapped a hand over her mouth, not wanting to waken Bobby, but unable to control the giggles that bubbled up inside her. "We can hire Edith Windslow as our public-relations woman. She can advertise for us not only here, but on Mars as well. I wonder if martians have ghosts?"

Laughter rumbled out of Forest. "I don't know," he said. "But I'll bet Edith does." They laughed uproariously, and when they finally calmed down, Julie looked at him helplessly, hopelessly. "This is going to be over soon, isn't it, Forest?" She heard the desperation in her own voice.

The pain was back in his eyes. "Yes," he said softly. "One way or the other, this is going to end soon." He scooted over next to her and placed an arm around her shoulder.

She leaned her head against him, needing his warmth to take away the chill pervading her bones. She released an exhausted sigh, wondering what Christopher had in store for them.

CHAPTER FOURTEEN

When Julie awakened the next morning, she knew what she needed to do. She woke up in front of the fireplace, to find Bobby still sleeping on the sofa and Forest nowhere in the room.

By the time she'd showered and changed clothes, Lottie had arrived and the scent of fresh coffee wafted through the air. Julie got Bobby up and told him to get dressed, then went into the kitchen.

"That coffee smells heavenly."

Lottie smiled, poured her a cup and set it before her at the table. "You want some breakfast? I could whip you up some eggs."

Julie shook her head. "No, thanks. I've got an errand to run. Have you seen Forest?"

Lottie nodded. "He's downstairs." She shook her head in bewilderment. "Said he's not going to the mill today. I asked him if he was sick, but he said he wasn't."

But, Julie knew he was sick, sick with the haunting of a little boy and afraid to leave her and Bobby alone, afraid that Christopher would somehow manage to lure them out into the woods.

By the time Julie had finished her coffee, Bobby appeared in the kitchen, dressed but still sleepy. "If

Forest comes up before we get back, tell him we're running errands and should be home in an hour or so," Julie told Lottie. Lottie nodded.

Minutes later, Julie and Bobby were in the car heading toward town. Julie hadn't wanted to tell Forest where she was going because she knew he'd think she'd lost her mind. And she probably had. But she couldn't sit idly by and wait for Christopher to reveal to them what he wanted. She didn't intend to endure another psychic battle like the one they had gone through the night before.

There was nothing more frightening in this world than knowing you had been touched by someone from the spirit world. Every time she thought of that moment in the kitchen when she'd felt those fingers encircle her wrist, she wanted to scream. Never in her life had she been so frightened.

It took her several minutes to find the address she sought, but she finally did. The house was nestled at the base of Kingsdon Hill. The house was small, but neat, with cream-colored shutters against pale blue aluminum siding. The front yard was oversized, the grass yellowed. She looked over at Bobby, who had fallen back asleep, and decided to leave him in the car.

She got out and locked Bobby in, then walked up to the front door. The place looked deserted. She hesitated before knocking, suddenly feeling enormously foolish for coming here. She could almost hear Lorna's laughter: "You needed help so you asked the town loon?" Julie pulled up the collar of her jacket, a chill of apprehension cooling the back of her neck.

Taking a deep breath, she knocked loudly. The door was instantly opened by Edith. "Good morning, dear. I've been expecting you," the old woman said, ushering her inside. "Told my friends I couldn't go with them this weekend because I was needed here."

Julie sat down in a chair next to the window, where she could look out and see Bobby. For a moment words failed her; she didn't even know where to begin. Why on earth had she come here?

"Well, spit it out, girl!" Edith exclaimed.

She took a deep breath. "You told me the other day that you sensed my son was in danger, that you knew I've been touched by the other side."

Edith nodded and eased herself down in a chair next to Julie. "Give me your hand," she demanded. Julie did as she asked. "Now tell me everything."

Julie did. She told the old woman about Christopher and Jeffrey and Forest. She held nothing back. She told of Forest's fears that he'd killed the child, of Christopher luring first Bobby, then her into the woods. She told Edith about Forest's blackouts, about him whispering the word *five*. Finally, with a trembling voice she scarcely recognized as her own, she told the old woman about the fingers clamping around her wrist and tugging her toward the back door.

When she was finished, Edith released her hand and leaned back in her chair, her brow deeply wrinkled in thought. She looked at Julie sharply. "You love Forest." It wasn't a question. It was a statement of fact, and Julie merely nodded.

"Did you come here today to see if I could tell you if he's innocent of the crime?"

"No." Julie felt a flush warm her face. "I know he isn't guilty. I—I know it in my heart."

Edith nodded, as if satisfied with her answer. "Well, it's easy to figure out why Christopher talks to Bobby. There's a blood connection there, and a strong psychic bond. But he's trying to communicate something...something important." Edith frowned once again. "It's odd. I don't sense any anger from the spirit of Christopher. I sense an aching loneliness. He's scared and so lonely."

"And that's what I've sensed from him," Julie agreed, remembering the deep, abiding loneliness that evoked tears in her each time she felt it. "But Forest thinks he wants revenge, that he is dangerous."

"Forest is blinded to everything but his own feelings of guilt. He's a danger only to himself," Edith replied without hesitation. "Forest haunts himself much more than Christopher does. His feelings of guilt will destroy him long before Christopher will."

Fear suddenly shot through Julie as she remembered Forest's promise that this would all be over soon. She'd seen the black despair that obscured all else in his eyes. Somewhere inside, she'd feared the choices he'd make in order to appease what he thought was Christopher's hunger for revenge.

"I've got to go," she said, rising from the chair with a sense of urgency. "I've got to get back home. I've got to get back to him."

Edith walked her to the door, sorrow etched in her lined face. "It's a sad, sad thing," she said, shaking her head. "A man in torment and a little boy whose body has never been properly buried. That poor little boy, so lost, so alone in the woods. Such a sad, sad thing." She gave Julie a quick hug. "You come back if you need me again. Just don't forget—most weekends I'm with my friends on the mother ship."

Julie thanked the woman, then raced to her car, her heart pounding with dread as Edith's words whirled around and around in her head. Forest was in danger from himself. She knew exactly what Edith meant. Would Forest take his own life in an effort to appease the ghostly demands of Christopher?

"Oh, please, no," she said softly. Surely he wouldn't do anything so drastic, so final. And yet, as she remembered his desperation, his resignation when he'd promised it would all be over soon, her heart lurched in fear.

"Mom?" Bobby awoke as they pulled up in front of the house.

"Bobby, I want you to go into the kitchen and stay with Lottie," Julie said, trying to keep the panic out of her voice. "She'll fix you some breakfast."

"What are you gonna do?" Bobby asked, obviously feeling the tension coming from her.

"I need to have a talk with Uncle Forest."

Minutes later Julie walked down the stairs to the basement, relieved to hear the sounds of Forest working. Without knocking, she walked into the room. He turned around, a smile lifting his lips. "Good morning," he said.

"I love you." The words slipped out of her mouth before she knew they were even in her mind. He stared at her blankly. She flushed hotly, but realized she'd already thrown caution to the wind. "I don't expect a reply. I don't expect you to reciprocate. I just need you to know that I love you." Her voice shook with a sudden flare of anger. "Forest Kingsdon, if you ever do anything to hurt yourself, I'll find you, either in heaven or hell. I'll hunt you down, and I'll haunt you like you've never been haunted before." She drew in a deep breath and released it with a shudder, emotionally spent by her outburst. "I—I just wanted you to know that," she finally said, then turned to leave.

Forest watched her go. She loved him. Her words should have granted him enormous joy, for he realized now that he loved her, too. He loved her as he'd never before loved a woman—with his heart, with his soul. But it was a murderer's heart and a blackened soul, and it was a love that had no future.

He sat down on the stool in front of the workbench, staring blankly at the carving he still held in his hand. So, she'd guessed about his final, ultimate option to quiet the ghost of Christopher. A whisper of a smile touched the corners of his mouth. She'd hunt him down in heaven or hell. Didn't she realize he was already in hell?

He sighed and set the chunk of wood down on the bench, his thoughts, his heart still consumed with Julie. She and Bobby had brought life back into this house, something that had been missing for a long time. But no amount of love could bring life back to him. He was damned, damned by evil blackouts that had already caused the death of one child. How long would Julie's love for him last if he had another blackout and Bobby disappeared just like Christopher? How long before Christopher's demand for justice really did drive him over the edge and into complete insanity?

"She'll find another man to love," he whispered to himself, the words causing an arrow of pain to stab him in the chest. She was young and attractive and had the kind of passion that demanded the same in return. Eventually she would find a man, a whole man who could give her the kind of love she needed. Julie was a survivor, and she would survive this heartache and eventually move on.

He didn't know how long he'd been sitting at the bench when he felt it . . . the familiar cold. It brought with it the smell of fallen trees and shadowy brush. Christopher.

"No." Forest tensed as he felt the well-known darkness reaching out for him. He gripped the edge of the workbench. As always, he fought against it, trying desperately to cling to consciousness. The cold intensified, surrounded him, crawled inside him. "No," he whispered again, fighting with all his mental capabilities. But the darkness grew, expanded and swallowed him whole.

* * *

Julie went from the basement to her bedroom, leaving instructions for Bobby, who was eating breakfast, to come up when he finished his meal.

In the bedroom, she picked up the wooden falcon, tears blurring her vision. She sank down on the bed, her fingers stroking the lines of the carved bird, her heart aching with her love for Forest.

It was tragic, all of it—Christopher's death, Forest's guilt, her love for him. Tragic that there seemed to be no answers, no resolution. How long could they exist in this house, being bombarded by a little ghost? How long could she stay, loving Forest and knowing there was no future, no hope?

She placed the falcon back on the dresser, her mind replaying her conversation with Edith. She didn't know what she had expected from the old woman. She'd hoped for answers, but should have known Edith would have no more answers than they did. *A little boy whose body has never been properly buried...* Edith's last words lingered in her mind and she frowned. The loneliness, the feeling of abandonment—those weren't the emotions of a ghost wanting revenge. They were the emotions of a little boy whose body had never been found, a little boy who was lost in the woods.

"My God," she gasped softly. Christopher wasn't trying to avenge his murder. He was trying to help them find him. As soon as she thought it, she knew it was true. It felt intrinsically right. Five. Five. What did it mean? Five yards? Five miles? Five what? She had to tell Forest. Damn it, why hadn't she realized it before?

She left the bedroom and hurried down the stairs. As she entered the kitchen, she paused and looked curiously at Lottie. "Where's Bobby?" she asked.

Lottie shrugged. "I went into the laundry room, and when I came back, he was gone. I assumed he'd gone upstairs with you."

Julie's breath caught painfully in her chest. "No, he didn't." She fought against the dread that lodged in her throat. Maybe he'd gone upstairs to the bathroom and she'd just missed him when she'd come down. Don't panic, she told herself calmly. She went to the bottom of the stairs and called his name. No reply. The silence was deafening. Where was Bobby? The dread that had lodged in her throat exploded into full-blown panic. Running back to the kitchen, she went to the stairs that led down to the basement. "Forest?" she cried. Again the silence screamed at her, and she knew with gut certainty that Forest was no longer in the basement. Where was he? Where was Bobby?

She dashed back into the kitchen and to the back door, icy terror gripping her. She stared at the woods and knew they were there...someplace in the dark woods with Christopher.

Without thought, she ran toward the woods, sobs of terror ripping through her. She crashed through the brush, unmindful of the thorns and brambles that reached for her, scratched at her. She knew only the need to find Bobby, find Forest.

"Julie?"

She broke into the clearing and fell toward Forest. He caught her by the shoulders. "Julie, what's wrong?" he asked urgently.

"It's Bobby. He's gone."

Forest dropped his hands from her, a look of dawning horror suffusing his features. "Oh, God...oh, please, no." He stared at Julie in abject panic. "I—I just had a blackout." He grabbed his head with both hands, his eyes wild with torment. "Oh, my God, what have I done? What in God's name have I done?"

Julie stared at him. Her heart thundered so loudly it seemed to fill the clearing. Forest had had a blackout and Bobby had disappeared. Ten years before he'd had a blackout when Christopher disappeared. Her head screamed with the implications, but her heart couldn't accept it. "No," she whispered. She'd seen what he did in his blackouts. He didn't turn into an evil monster. There was no evil inside him. "Forest, you haven't done anything. What we have to do right now is find Bobby."

"It's just like before," Forest said tonelessly. "It's just like when Christopher disappeared. It's all happening again."

She grabbed his arm and jerked it impatiently. "That doesn't matter right now. What's important is Bobby. We have to find him."

Forest looked at her, and slowly some of the horror in his eyes dissipated. "Yes...yes, we've got to find him. We've got to find him."

Together they left the clearing, stomping through the woods and calling his name over and over again. Lottie joined them in the search until she tired, then she went back to the house in case Bobby should show up there.

As the minutes passed and they walked deeper and deeper into the woods, Julie fought against hysteria. Forest was like a man possessed, calling Bobby's name over and over again until his voice was hoarse. She felt his torment but could do nothing to assuage it. She couldn't do anything but pray for Bobby. Where was he? Where was her baby?

They'd searched for over an hour when despair finally gained possession of Julie. She sank down onto a fallen log and sobbed. "The woods are too big. There's too much timber," she cried. Forest sat down beside her, her despair echoed in the hollowness of his eyes.

"Maybe he's not out here," Forest offered without conviction.

Julie shook her head. "He's here. I feel him." She squeezed her eyes shut. "He's someplace in these woods and he's scared and alone...just like Christopher." Her eyes flew open as she remembered what had brought her out of her bedroom in the first place. "We need to go back to the clearing," she said with conviction. "Christopher has been trying to tell us something, and that's the place you always go when you're in one of your blackouts."

They backtracked to the clearing. Once there Julie stood and looked around. "Five," she said softly.

"Five is what he wanted us to know. But five what?" She looked at Forest in frustration. "Forest, Christopher doesn't want revenge. He wants to be found. He's been lost in these woods for ten years. He wants us to find him."

Forest gazed at her helplessly. "But how?"

"Listen." Julie tilted her head, then froze. Drifting on the air was the sound of pitiful sobbing. "Bobby!" she cried, all other thoughts fleeing from her mind. "Bobby, where are you?"

"Julie." Forest grabbed her upper arms and held her in a viselike grip. "Julie, that's not Bobby. Listen, it's Christopher."

She hesitated and knew he was right. Cold air encased her, sweeping over her with the icy breath of an open grave. The childish sobbing ripped at her heart, ached deep inside her, and tears began to fall from her eyes. "I—I have to go," she said, struggling to free herself from his grasp. "I have to...I need to go." She stumbled free from him.

"No, don't." Forest's fear deepened his voice and he grabbed her arm once again. "It could be a trick. He could be luring you to your death."

She shook her head vehemently. She reached up and touched the side of Forest's face. "We've been so frightened by him. We've been fighting against him all along. The thing we've forgotten is that he's just a little boy. He's a scared little boy who is lost." She broke away from Forest and headed down the path, toward the sound of the cries.

"Julie, come back," Forest called from behind her, but she couldn't stop now. The crying possessed her completely. She was surrounded by it and succumbed to it, allowing it to lead her where it wanted her to go.

The whimpers pulled her down an unfamiliar path, one that was narrow and steep, with deep ravines on either side. There was no sunlight on this path, only dark shadows and the scent of rich earth and green vines. As she passed each crevasse, she subconsciously kept count.

The cries grew louder, more intense, like the wind howling mournfully about the eaves of a house. Only this wind was inside her, its sorrow deep in her heart. She not only heard the cries, she felt them, around her, inside her. She was vaguely aware of Forest just behind her, finding the narrow path difficult to maneuver because of his bigger size. And still the cries drew her onward.

It was as she reached the fifth ravine that the cries seemed to explode in her head. She stopped, her heart thudding anxiously, and looked over the side. The sides plunged steeply downward, the bottom too dark to see.

She took a step closer and screamed as she felt the moist earth lip give way beneath her feet. Flailing her arms wildly, she fought for balance. Feeling only empty air, she heard Forest's impotent cry as she fell.

She plunged down the hillside, her body gaining momentum as she rolled, sticks and brush flattening beneath her. She finally came to rest at the bottom. For a moment she remained perfectly still, waiting for the pain of broken bones and bruises to assault her. There was no immediate ache, so she cautiously sat up.

"Julie?" Forest cried from above, his voice tortured beyond comprehension. "Julie?" he sobbed.

"I'm all right," she yelled back. "It's okay."

"Mom?" The small voice came from her left, and in the murky darkness that surrounded her, she saw Bobby sitting on the ground.

"Oh, baby," she cried, hurrying over to him and pulling him into her arms. "Are you all right?"

"I fell. I hurt my ankle. I can't walk on it." Bobby sobbed and held on to her. "I couldn't get up. I was so scared."

"Shh, it's all right now," Julie said, hugging him close.

"Julie?" Forest yelled again, his tone frantic. She realized he couldn't see what she was doing, didn't know that Bobby was with her.

"It's okay, Forest. Bobby's here."

"Is he all right?"

"I think so. He's fine. We're going to come up." Julie stood and helped Bobby to his feet. He cried out as his right foot touched the ground. She leaned forward and raised his pant leg. His ankle was already swollen. It was either broken or badly sprained. "Put your arm around my waist and lean against me," she instructed.

They took a step forward, but stopped as Julie's foot stumbled over something. She started to kick whatever it was out of her way, then stopped, horror sweeping through her. Beside her foot, half-covered with leaves, was what looked to be a bone. She swept the leaves away and realized there was an entire skeleton.

"Forest, you'd better come down here," she said with unnatural calm.

"What's wrong?"

She took a deep breath, then answered, "I think we just found Christopher."

CHAPTER FIFTEEN

"Okay?" Julie asked Bobby. He was resting on the sofa, his sprained ankle professionally taped by the doctor who had just left.

It had been a crazy afternoon. Forest had descended into the ravine and helped her carry Bobby out. They'd come right back to the house and had called the sheriff and the doctor. Within minutes the driveway had been filled with cars, and Forest took the sheriff, his men and the county coroner to the ravine where Christopher's body was.

"Mom?"

"What, honey?" Julie asked, stroking a strand of Bobby's dark hair away from his forehead.

"Are you mad at me?" The boy's eyes filled with tears. "I didn't mean to go, but Christopher was crying and I just wanted to help him."

"Oh, honey, I'm not mad." She gathered him into her arms and held him close, tears filling her eyes as she realized again how very close she'd come to losing him. "I was scared when we couldn't find you."

"I was afraid you wouldn't be able to find me, but Christopher said he'd bring you to me. He did, didn't he?"

Julie thought of the child's cries that had led her through the twisted undergrowth, down that narrow path. "Yes, Christopher led me right to where you were. He wanted you to be okay, and he wanted us to find him."

She released Bobby and stood up as Forest came into the room. "They just took him away," he said. He sank down on the chair, a look of bewilderment on his face.

"Forest?"

"They've ruled his death accidental. It appears that he must have fallen off the trail and into the ravine. When he fell, he hit his head on a rock and that's what killed him. The rock was still there, under his head."

"I told you," she said softly, a rush of relief sweeping through her. "I told you that you couldn't be responsible." She searched his face, looking for some sign of inner peace, some elation at the knowledge that he hadn't been responsible for Christopher's death. But his eyes were dark, enigmatic.

"Uncle Forest?"

Forest looked at Bobby.

"You don't have to be sad anymore. Christopher is happy now. He told me so," Bobby explained.

Forest frowned and stepped closer. "What did he tell you?"

"He told me he just wanted us to find him. He didn't like it in the woods all by himself. He just wanted to play hide-and-seek, but he fell off the trail." Bobby hesitated. "He said something else, too, but it didn't make any sense."

"What?" Forest asked, his voice edged with tension.

"He said to tell the falcon that the crow loves him."

Forest's face crumbled and tears filled his eyes. With a curt nod, he left the living room.

"Did I say something wrong?" Bobby asked worriedly.

"No, honey, you said something very right," Julie assured him. Leaning down, she quickly kissed his forehead. "I'll be right back." She hurried into the kitchen, where Forest sat at the table, his head buried in his arms.

Julie sat down beside him, touching his head so he'd know she was there. He cried, and Julie understood that, for the first time, he wasn't crying for Christopher, he wasn't crying from guilt. This time his tears were for himself, and for the ten years he'd spent hating himself. He cried for the man he might have been, the things he might have done, the people he might have loved except for the burden of his guilt. She knew they were tears that would finally heal him.

He didn't cry for long, and when he finally raised his head, she saw that the haunted look gone from his eyes. "It's really over, isn't it?" he asked hoarsely.

She nodded. "Yes, I think it's finally over."

He rubbed a hand across his forehead. "There's no way Bobby would know that Christopher used to call me Falcon. It was a game between us—the falcon and the crow." He rubbed his forehead again. "There's something I still don't understand. The blackouts."

"I think I do. I think every time you blacked out it was because Christopher was trying to contact you— and you felt overwhelmed by your worry, your concern for him, your love, your guilt. The feelings on both sides were so powerful that they sort of short-circuited your nervous system and you couldn't respond normally."

He frowned. "But what about that first time...the day Christopher disappeared?"

She reached across the table and took his hand. "Forest, I think when you had that first blackout Christopher was already dead. It would take only a moment for an energetic little boy to reach that ravine and fall, and you told me he could run like the wind. He died instantly and tried to contact you at once."

Forest nodded, accepting her explanation. It made as much sense as anything. He looked at her hand enclosed in his, felt her love radiating toward him. It stunned him, the total realization of her love. But it was too soon. His head was filled with the overwhelming events of the day.

He gently removed his hand from hers. "I—I think I need some time alone."

Julie nodded and watched as he disappeared down the stairs to his workroom. She didn't know what she had expected, what she'd anticipated. All she knew was what she'd wanted—to see the haunted look gone from his eyes. For him to take her in his arms and tell her he loved her. But perhaps he didn't.

She closed her eyes, fighting against the heartache that thought brought with it. At least his pain was finally over, and perhaps that alone could be enough for her. Perhaps . . . but she didn't think so.

Julie watched Forest as he leaned over and placed a hand on the newly erected headstone. Christopher now rested not only beside his mother, but with Richard and Jeffrey as well. Forest had paid to have Jeffrey's body moved here, to the Kingsdon Cemetery, where the family could rest together.

It had been two weeks since Julie had fallen into the ravine and found Christopher. It was amazing how quickly everything had returned to normal. Bobby had gone back to school with tales of a ghost boy who'd needed to be found. His story, along with his bandaged ankle, had made him something of a hero with his classmates.

Forest had gone back to working long hours at the mill, then closing himself off in his workroom. He kept himself distant, detached from everything and everyone. And Julie went back to work at the newspaper office and tried to forget that she loved him.

Now, as she watched him saying his final goodbyes to the little boy he had loved and lost, her love for him was a physical pain in her chest. He'd never made any promises, but she had so hoped . . .

"Mom?" Bobby tugged lightly on her coat.

"What, honey?" She turned to him and pulled his collar up more tightly around his neck. It was a raw day, with the promise of snow in the air.

"Are we going to live here forever?"

Julie hesitated and looked back at Forest. He'd been so distant, had kept himself so isolated the last two weeks. She wondered now if his passion for her, the desire that had burned so hotly and drawn him to her, had just been a result of the strange experiences they had shared. Perhaps it had been only his desperation that had caused him to reach out to her. Desperation, not love.

"Mom?"

Bobby pulled her from her thoughts, reminding her that he was waiting for an answer. "I don't know, Bobby. Forever is a long time," she finally answered. "Would you like to stay here in Kingsdon?"

He nodded vigorously. "I want to stay right where we are." He looked over to where Forest still remained by the graves. "We've got family here, Mom. We've got roots."

She smiled, remembering how on the drive from New York she'd kept telling him that—that they were going to Kingsdon because they had roots there... family. No matter how her heart ached for Forest, she couldn't be sorry they'd come. Bobby had found what he needed here, and no matter where they went, Bobby would have those roots.

Forest stood up and walked back to where she and Bobby stood, his face radiating a peace that soothed her aching heart. To Julie's surprise, Bobby immediately reached for his hand. "It's okay now, Uncle Forest. Christopher is happy now. And we can all be happy, too."

Forest nodded, his gaze on Julie. "Yes, I think it's time we all find some happiness now."

"Hey, it's snowing," Bobby announced. Sure enough large flakes were drifting down from the overcast sky.

"Come on, we'd better get back up the hill before the roads get slick," Forest said. Together they got into the car and drove back up the hill to Kingsdon Manor.

An hour later Julie stood at her bedroom window, staring out at the swirling snow, which now covered the ground and was rapidly piling up. Lorna had warned her that winters here could be harsh, and she had a feeling this would be the harshest one she'd ever known. The thought of being snowed in with Forest, of having to hide her love, endure his distance, was devastating.

"Julie?"

She turned at the sound of Forest's deep voice. He stood in the doorway, his gaze dark and enigmatic. "Can I talk to you for a minute?"

"Of course." She hoped her emotions weren't there on her face to be seen. He'd been burdened with unnecessary guilt for so long. She didn't want to burden him now with her love. He'd probably come to ask her how much longer they were going to stay. He'd never wanted them here in the first place, she reminded herself.

"Where's Bobby?" he asked curiously as he stepped into the room.

"He's downstairs in the kitchen with Lottie. They were going to make some hot chocolate."

He nodded and walked over to where she stood, his eyes still not revealing anything of his inner thoughts. "They say we might get a foot of snow by morning."

"Lorna told me the winters could be long here." Julie's mouth was dry. He stood too close to her and offered her nothing. "Did you come here to talk about the weather?"

He smiled. "No, actually, I came here to talk about heaven and hell."

She frowned. "Heaven and hell?"

He nodded and took another step toward her. She stepped back, feeling the cold panes of the window behind her.

"You really would have hunted me down in heaven or hell?" he asked.

She realized what he was talking about and felt a hot flush sweep over her face. "I was frightened for you when I said that."

"And what about the other part?" He stood so close to her that his heat warmed her front as efficiently as the window cooled her back. "Did you say you loved me only because you were frightened for me?"

"No. I said it because I meant it." Her heart thundered in her chest, so loud she was certain he must hear it.

He tilted his head, his gaze soft as it rested on her face. "How...how could you love me?" he asked incredulously.

She sighed, her heart aching with her love. She reached up and placed a hand on his cheek. "Oh, Forest, how could I not?" She removed her hand and turned to stare out the window, unsure what he wanted from her, what he was willing to give in return. "It's funny, Jeffrey was charming and so easy to fall in love with, but it was so difficult to stay in love with him. You...you were difficult to fall in love with, but..." She turned and looked at him once again, this time knowing her feelings were in her eyes, knowing she was unable to hide the intensity of her love for him. "I think I will always love you."

He groaned and pulled her to him, his lips capturing hers in a kiss that stole her breath, banished the cold of the window and surrounded her with heat. "Oh, Julie, I love you," he said when their kiss ended. "I love you so much it frightens me."

Tears trembled on her lashes as she clung to him. "I've been so afraid. You've been so distant, so aloof since we found Christopher."

He led her over to the bed and they sat down. "I had to be sure," he said softly. He touched a strand of her hair, then cupped her chin. "I had to be sure the blackouts were really gone, that all this was truly over." He released her face, his eyes still warm and tender as he gazed at her. "It wasn't until today, at the cemetery, that I knew it really was over. I know it sounds crazy, but I felt Christopher's peace and knew it was all going to be okay. But it won't be okay without you."

Julie's heart exploded with happiness and tears once again sparkled in her eyes. "I was afraid I'd have to leave here, leave you. I couldn't have stayed here, loving you silently."

"If you ever leave me I'll hunt you down, whether in heaven or hell. I'll hunt you down and haunt you like you've never been haunted before."

Julie laughed with abandon. "I think one haunting is quite enough for me." Her laughter died and her love once again surged up within her. "I'll never leave you, Forest. You're part of my heart, my soul. I wouldn't be alive without you."

"Then you'll marry me?" he asked, his body tense, his eyes momentarily dark with anxiety. "Julie, I want to marry you and be a father to Bobby. I want us to fill this house with laughter and love."

"Oh, yes, Forest. Yes." Again his lips met hers, and in his kiss she heard his promise of tomorrow, the promise of forever.

When their kiss ended, he pulled her up. "Come on, let's go tell Lottie and Bobby." He frowned for a moment, his gaze going out the window, where the snow obscured any view. "We might have to wait until spring for a honeymoon."

"No, we won't," Julie said with an impish smile. "I'm sure if we talked to Edith she could get us booked on one of her weekend flights."

Forest laughed, the rich, full sound embracing Julie. "Or we could just stay here and be snowed in for the winter." His eyes burned hotly and a shiver of delight raced up her spine.

"I suddenly have a feeling that winter won't be long enough," she said. As she looked at him, saw the beauty of his features freed from torment, the promise of his love so bold, so pure in his eyes, she knew he was finally the man she'd always known he could be. A good, loving, gentle man. And she knew their love would last through good times and bad...through heaven and hell.

*　*　*　*　*

Welcome To The
Dark Side Of Love...

COMING NEXT MONTH

#62 TRUST ME—Charlotte Moore

An eerie green mist... The smell of decaying flowers...
Margo Stafford didn't know why the mortuary-turned-
shelter scared her so, but she sensed its evil to her very
core. Kane Rainer was the only sign of sanity amid insane surroundings, so she reached out to him with open arms.
And though this riveting, reclusive man told her he couldn't—
shouldn't—be trusted, Margo was already too far gone.

COMING IN TWO MONTHS

#63 OLD FLAMES—Sandra Dark

James Shockley had no idea he'd been living above an unholy
burial ground, one Dr. Amber Sheridan called the find of a
lifetime. But James found nothing earth-shattering about the
age-old crypt, while everything Amber did or said struck a
chord within him. She seemed eerily familiar, sensually
provocative. And as a strange darkness gripped at his soul,
James knew his desire for Amber was both destined—and
dangerous....

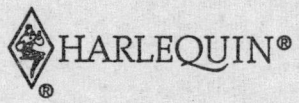

Yo amo novelas con corazón!

Starting this March, Harlequin opens up to a whole new world of readers with two new romance lines in SPANISH!

Harlequin Deseo
* passionate, sensual and exciting stories

Harlequin Bianca
* romances that are fun, fresh and very contemporary

With four titles a month, each line will offer the same wonderfully romantic stories that you've come to love—now available in Spanish.

Look for them at selected retail outlets.

HARLEQUIN®

SPANT

Bestselling author

RACHEL LEE

takes her Conard County series to new heights with

A CONARD COUNTY Reckoning

This March, Rachel Lee brings readers a brand-new, longer-length, out-of-series title featuring the characters from her successful Conard County miniseries.

Janet Tate and Abel Pierce have both been betrayed and carry deep, bitter memories. Brought together by great passion, they must learn to trust again.

"Conard County is a wonderful place to visit! Rachel Lee has crafted warm, enchanting stories. These are wonderful books to curl up with and read. I highly recommend them."
—*New York Times* bestselling author
Heather Graham Pozzessere

Available in March, wherever Silhouette books are sold.

INTRODUCING...

A collection of award-winning books by award-winning
authors! From Harlequin and Silhouette.

Heaven In Texas
by Curtiss Ann Matlock

National Reader's Choice Award Winner—
Long Contemporary Romance

Let Curtiss Ann Matlock take you to a place called
Heaven In Texas, where sexy cowboys in well-worn jeans
are the answer to every woman's prayer!

"Curtiss Ann Matlock blends reality with romance
to perfection!"
—*Romantic Times*

Available this March wherever Silhouette books are sold.

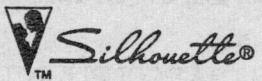

WC-3

HOW MUCH IS THAT COUPLE IN THE WINDOW?
by Lori Herter

Book 1 of Lori's Million-Dollar Marriages miniseries
Yours Truly™—February

Salesclerk Jennifer Westgate's new job is to live in a department store display window for a week as the bride of a gorgeous groom. Here's what sidewalk shoppers have to say about them:

"Why is the window so steamy tonight? I can't see what they're doing!" —Henrietta, age 82

"That mousey bride is hardly Charles Derring's type. It's me who should be living in the window with him!" —Delphine, Charles's soon-to-be ex-girlfriend

"Jennifer never modeled pink silk teddies for me! This is an outrage!" —Peter, Jennifer's soon-to-be ex-boyfriend

"How much is that couple in the window?" —Timmy, age 9

HOW MUCH IS THAT COUPLE IN THE WINDOW? by Lori Herter—Book 1 of her Million-Dollar Marriages miniseries—available in February from

Love—when you least expect it!